Clemenceau's Daughters
A Novel

Rocky Porch Moore

Published by:
Southern Yellow Pine (SYP) Publishing
4351 Natural Bridge Rd.
Tallahassee, FL 32305

www.syppublishing.com

This is a work of fiction. Names, characters, places, and events that occur either are the products of the author's imagination or are used fictitiously. Any resemblance to actual persons, places, or events is purely coincidental.

The contents and opinions expressed in this book do not necessarily reflect the views and opinions of Southern Yellow Pine Publishing, nor does the mention of brands or trade names constitute endorsement.

ISBN-10: 194086965X
ISBN-13: 978-1-940869-65-0
ISBN-13: ePub 978-1-940869-66-7
ISBN-13: Adobe eBook 978-1-940869-67-4
Library of Congress Control Number: 2015956580

Printed in the United States of America
First Edition
December 2015

Acknowledgements

This is a work of fiction. It is not a memoir. The setting, however, is very much autobiographical and reflects my childhood home as accurately as memory, and the psyche of a precocious girl, which I attempt to capture, allow. The characters and events are my inventions and do not directly parallel relationships I experienced, but rather reflect the tendency of the past to cling to the present, both personally and societally. The family saga belongs to the characters; it is not my own.

I thank Lon and Linda Porch for being the solid foundation that the parents I created for the young narrator are not. I remember our home on July Mountain fondly, haints and all.

This book would not be possible without the unwavering support of Russ Moore, who has urged me to "go for it" for a quarter century. After four children, two farms, and many a school year, I finally listened.

I would also like to express my gratitude to Terri Gerrell and Southern Yellow Pine Publishing for helping me bring my vision to fruition. I thank Melisa Taylor, who offered both encouragement and much-needed criticism in tightening the narrative.

Finally, thanks to Anna and my students for all your encouragement.

In memory of Linda

Preface

They say the sins of the fathers can be visited upon the sons through seven generations. The sins of the mothers know no such bounds. They are nurtured, protected, and handed down from generation to generation, world without end. They are inescapable and liberating, choking and cathartic, tomorrow and yesterday. These sins are an unspoken blood legacy, and though they may be forgiven in the eyes of man—and perhaps even those of God—the daughters are never truly cleansed. Their blood is tainted, an earthy rot just this side of perception. The sins remain across oceans, across time, across life, across death. As palpable as a heartbeat, as quiet as a still-soft voice, they are as present as a soul. They abide. They bide.

Book One

Daughter

1

The tree was old, Mommy said, older than even Mama's mama, which was about as old as Debbie could imagine. It might even be as old as America, but it was hard to believe something like a tree could have lived that long. Debbie knew trees themselves were as old as the earth. They grew even before people were God-breathed into the living world. She was five years old and could read whole books all by herself. Her favorites were a set of children's Bible stories she had received from Aunt Edna, the schoolteacher. Mommy had said Aunt Edna's gifts would always have to do with school, and that suited Debbie just fine. She would get to go to school when summer ended. She'd be younger than the other first graders, but Daddy told her it would be okay because she would be smarter anyhow.

The Bible stories had beautiful, colored pictures that Debbie pretended she could walk around inside. Some of the pictures were scary, but Debbie would pretend inside them just the same. There was a picture of a beautiful tree in the garden, even more beautiful than her tree in the back yard, a ball's throw from the porch steps. This was the illustration she loved most.

Debbie remembered things. She remembered things that Daddy said and things that Mommy said. She remembered things she heard other grownups say. But, most of all, she remembered things she read. When she closed her eyes, the stories unfolded like a movie inside her head. She sat down in the well of her tree, where the heat of the Alabama summer couldn't quite stretch its fingers, and she watched her stories. Fat Sarah, the woman who kept Debbie while Mommy and Daddy were away at work, watched her stories on the TV every afternoon. They were silly and full of kissing doctors and nurses. Debbie was always glad when Fat Sarah sent her out the back door with a cheese sandwich and orders to stay out of the road.

If Debbie hugged her knees up to her chest, she could disappear into the embrace of the tree. The hollow of the oak was just the right size for a little girl, and she traced patterns in the cool dirt as she sat. Mommy and Daddy were too big to fit and too old to feel the magic of the tree. Debbie didn't really believe in magic. She knew most, if not all of it, was just tricks, but there was something about the tree that made her feel safe.

"Why you want to sit in that musty old tree is beyond me," Mommy fussed. "You'd better watch out for snakes and spiders up in that hollow. They want to get out of the heat just as much as anybody else. If you get bit, you're going to get a whipping to boot."

It was when she was sweeping about the hollow with a big stick to make sure no spiders were creeping in the shadows that Debbie found the cache. She almost lost her stick when it plunged into a hole in the upper shaded recesses. She'd never noticed it before, but then again, she'd never really poked all around the higher parts of the hollow. She threw down the stick and ran back into the house to grab Daddy's flashlight. Up the back steps she flew and was in such a hurry, she let the screen door slam behind her.

"You get back outside and play!" called Fat Sarah from the living room. "My story's still on. And stay out of that road!"

"Yes, Miss Sarah," called Debbie dutifully. She had enough sense to know that calling her babysitter Fat Sarah to her face would get her a whipping for sure, even if Mommy and

Daddy both called the sitter Fat Sarah any time she was out of hearing.

Fat Sarah was poor white trash. Debbie figured that meant she didn't have enough money for a car. Every morning before work, Daddy drove across town to pick up Fat Sarah. He brought her back to the house so that she could cook breakfast for the family before the grownups had to leave.

What Mommy and Daddy didn't know was that Fat Sarah cooked another breakfast for herself once they were on their way, only she called it snack time. Fat Sarah would set Debbie to looking at her Bible story books or watching Captain Kangaroo while she fried up potatoes and onions, bacon, and eggs. She'd play the radio while she cooked, singing along to the Gospel Hour in a voice that sounded a lot like Daddy's Patsy Cline vinyl record—mostly clear with scratchy spots here and there—while she dished up a hearty snack for herself. All traces of Fat Sarah's morning snack went in either her belly or to GodLutherYouStink the Saint Bernard.

"You need to always be on good terms with the family dog, Debbie," advised Fat Sarah, "even one as godforsaken as that beast. That way the dog will help you if you ever come calling in a time of need."

Debbie didn't really mind the dog getting a plate because she abhorred breakfast. She didn't even like the smell of it. Fat Sarah knew this and handed Debbie a chocolate bar from the recesses of her black patent pocketbook. "You need to always be on good terms with little girls, too," she simpered. "That way the little girl will love you and keep your secrets. After all, a secret loses half its power if it isn't shared."

Debbie knew Fat Sarah's secret was that she was eating the family's food, but the chocolate bars seemed to make it okay. She didn't love Fat Sarah but tolerated her well enough on account of they were both naughty, but it was worse when a grownup was naughty. Who could blame a little girl for liking candy? Plus, she believed Fat Sarah when she bent down low and looked Debbie straight in the eyes. Fat Sarah's voice was barely above a whisper, but Debbie knew she was speaking the truth. Her eyes looked inside her with an intensity that made Debbie believe Fat Sarah could see her every fear and share her every secret whether Debbie wanted to or not.

"Debbie, I give you the chocolate to shut your mouth. If you tell your mommy and daddy what I cook and what I do, I will tell the Man on the Mountain to come down here. I will tell him to eat your baby brother…, and he will, because the Man on the Mountain is my kin."

Debbie's eyes grew big as she glanced at the bassinet where Brent lay sleeping. But Fat Sarah didn't stop there. Her words dripped sweet as honey from her mouth, but what she said was poison.

"Yes, you know about the Man on the Mountain. Don't you? He comes into your dreams. I can summon him to come down off the mountain like a shadow or like an angry wind. I can call him. He can take whoever he chooses. It could be that babe sleeping over there. It could be your daddy or your mommy. It could be you. Just you remember that, Little Debbie, and you keep our secrets sealed up sweetly inside. Now, take this candy bar and go sit in that tree of yours for a while." Fat Sarah's mouth smiled, but her eyes did not, even when she started singing "One Day at a Time, Sweet Jesus" along with the Gospel Hour.

Debbie was shaking but obediently took the candy bar and wobbled unsteadily down the back steps. She glanced to her left, past the road and up to the mountain rising beside the little green house that had been pleasant until now. A large cloud cast its shadow on the mountainside, and as it floated across the sky, its shadow crept down the mountain toward her. She squealed and made for the cranny in her oak tree trunk. Debbie slid in and pulled up her knees to hug her legs tightly to her. And she cried.

It seemed like a long time before she heard the scrape of the screen door and Fat Sarah call out, "Debbie, come on in, and get your lunch," just as sweet as you please with no hint of the evil that had come out minutes before. Or was it hours? She wasn't sure. She might have been sleeping. She wanted to believe she had dreamt Fat Sarah's words, but the threat was just as real as the candy bar in her lap. Somehow, sitting in the cool of the tree's embrace had comforted her, though. Shadow can't swallow shadow, child. I stand sentinel. The Mountain has eyes. The Mountain has eyes. Shadow can't swallow shadow.

Whether it was a thought or a voice or a feeling, Debbie really couldn't tell, but she rose and walked resolutely to the back steps with only a furtive glance at the mountain rising over her like a green ocean wave. The chocolate bar lay like a forgotten offering in the cool of the oak tree.

2

The little, green house sat in Woods Cove in the elbow of two roads, both with the same name. The house faced the road that led to July Mountain, which although not large by Smoky Mountain standards, loomed over the cove, nevertheless, in a sort of fist, as if the mountain was a giant hand poised to smash whatever fell in its reach. The road that marked the west side of the property skirted alongside the foot of the mountain and wound its way in a lazy circle back to the mouth of the cove. From the lookout on the mountaintop, one could see that the circle really wasn't a circle at all. The roads formed more of a lowercase letter b with the stick of the b disappearing into the green of the mountain as it began to climb.

The cove was sparsely populated, but there were enclaves of family properties scattered about it where three or four houses or trailers had been built or hauled in as sons and daughters grew up and started families of their own. The families were tight-knit and protective of their land. Most of them had large dogs standing watch over what was theirs and an attitude that didn't exactly welcome newcomers or Sunday drivers. Where the circular part of the road ended beside the green house, there was a largely ignored stop sign.

The tiny house sat perilously close to both roads. The front yard was hard-packed dirt and had just enough room to pull a couple of cars up to the front porch. A good-sized spruce that butted up against a mature maple tree took up most of the rest of the front yard. The spruce was grossly misshapen from where the county had trimmed it off the power lines, swooping low across the corner to head down into the cove. Daddy wanted to cut down that tree, but Mommy wouldn't let him on account of it was probably somebody's Christmas tree a long, long time ago, and it was all that remained to remind us they were here. He said that since they were just renting the house anyway, it wasn't really his job to cut it, and if anybody got himself killed in a car wreck, it wouldn't be his fault. So the spruce survived. It was hard for a driver who was stopped to see his way clear past that spruce. Maybe that was why most of them didn't bother. They just gritted their teeth and made the turn, figuring anybody coming up the road would have time to stop. Besides, folks who lived in the cove pretty much agreed that the stop sign was more of a suggestion than a law, so they expected their neighbors to hop out blindly.

Trouble was, right up the road was a sharp curve that drivers liked to power through like NASCAR racers. After a little rise, the road started heading a bit downhill, and people just couldn't help but accelerate. By the time they approached the little, green house on the corner, they were either braking hard to make the turn or punching it to thrill to the way the asphalt rose just enough in the intersection to tickle their tummies.

Not only was the house situated close to the road in front of it, but it was equally close to the road beside it—so close, in fact, that Debbie wasn't allowed to even play in the side yard, which Daddy said was GodLutherYouStink's anyway. The huge dog, matted and tufted, tended to wriggle himself up under the house where he lay growling or snoring—Debbie wasn't sure which—with eyes glinting and fixed on the mountain. He was always chained, but Daddy had miscalculated the length of the chain, so GodLutherYouStink could stand a step or two on the blacktop if he had a mind to. This was usually on Saturday nights when he'd shimmy out from under the house, haunches oozy with drippings from a pipe that was either leaky or had

9

been gnawed loose, and play chicken with whoever happened to be cruising the cove.

Sunday mornings, the side yard was littered with beer cans the teenage boys and their daddies tossed out on their way home. At first, Mommy and Daddy just thought the whole cove was nothing but poor white trash, and Daddy called in the law to see if they would patrol on Saturday nights to keep people from chucking beer cans against the house and antagonizing the poor dog. The deputy they sent had family in Woods Cove. He tucked his thumbs in his belt loops and looked Daddy in the eye, even though he was down in the yard, and Daddy was standing up on the porch.

"Mr. Ballard," he began, addressing Daddy with all due respect, "them boys ain't really littering. It's just that the Howard women won't allow no beer drankin' on their land, being the God-fearing Christians they all are. Their men do their drinking before they get home. You see, Old Man Abby lived in this here green house for years and years. He walked Woods Cove Road every day, picking up cans and trading in the aluminum and glass bottles he come across to make his living. As he started to get on in years, they decided they'd save him the trouble and give him easy pickin's. They was practicing Christian charity."

"Well, Deputy, that old man don't live here no more. We do. And we don't need no charity, Christian or otherwise," Daddy replied with a frown.

"That may very well be, but old habits die hard, and they ain't hurtin' a thing. If I was you, I'd just pick up them cans and keep your dog on his chain if you ain't gonna build a fence. It's the neighborly thing. Besides, you don't want to be on the wrong side of the Howards when you're living here in Woods Cove. " The deputy turned on his heel and got in his car, clearly finished with the conversation. As he drove off, Daddy shook his head.

"What's this world coming to when the damn law sides with the trash? I ought to bag up every one of them damn beer cans and dump them right on the damn Howards' front porch. Then, we'll see how they damn well like it!"

But Daddy never did.

The house itself was old. It looked like it was built a long time ago, maybe in the 1940s. It looked like a house that could have lived in the Great Depression. She'd heard Nonny talk of hard times, and the house just seemed to fit the picture she'd imagined as she listened to the old tales. It was small and set up on piers so that dogs would have a cool place to lie. Mommy forbade Debbie from crawling up under the house, though, because that's where the rats and spiders lived. Mommy didn't want anything to do with rats, spiders, or snakes and tried to pass down a healthy fear of them.

A porch spanned the front of the house, which was just one room wide. The front door opened right into the living room. There wasn't a foyer or any sort of threshold. The houses on TV all had a sort of tiny room where visitors put their pocketbooks on a table. This house had no in between space. You were either outside on the porch or inside navigating around the TV console. In fact, if you rushed inside the front door, it slammed into the TV, and Daddy hollered words little girls oughtn't to hear. Try as she might to be careful, Debbie would whack the TV with that door. It was as if it jumped out of her hands. Daddy would cuss and start in about folks not building to code or some such nonsense but would end with Debbie snuggled into his lap as he watched and cussed at the local news.

Directly behind the living room was a small kitchen, and the house widened there to accommodate two bedrooms and a bathroom so tiny that Mommy joked about elbows and assholes. "Assholes" was one of those words on the list of things little girls shouldn't say but grownups could. Debbie couldn't wait to grow up and use any old word she pleased. A back door with steps led down to the giant oak tree, which took up most of the back yard, or at least the part that Daddy kept mowed.

North of the oak tree, the yard's boundary was a bank that dropped down into a weedy gully. Even Daddy said this was the perfect place for snakes. It bubbled a rusted, sulfuric-smelling mud and never dried up, even in the heat of summer. Daddy said that the septic tank was probably rusted plumb through, and that was the shit of the folks who used to live here's gift to us.

"I don't know what's worse, the shit or the damned sage," Daddy complained. "I've got a thing or two to say to our damned landlord." But he never did.

That stench was masked by the even more overpowering smell of sage, which grew prolifically along the embankment before fading into a tired-looking soybean field. This vista was presided over by a smaller oak from whose spindly limb hung a handmade swing built just for Debbie, even though she'd have to share it with Brent once he got big enough to ride on it.

Debbie's grandfather, Mommy's daddy, had built it for her shortly after they had moved into the little green house. He made the hour-long drive all the way from Morgan City, which really wasn't a city at all, just to hang it and watch her fly. It was the only time Papa ever visited their house although Debbie could remember lots of Sunday afternoons, sitting on Nonny and Papa's front porch, shelling peas and watching the traffic speed by on the highway. The swing was a sawn plank two feet long and three inches thick. It was bolted clean through to secure its metal handles. He used upholstery tacks to affix a leather cover to the seat, both to protect the lumber from wear and Debbie's rear end from splinters, despite his having sanded the edges. Debbie had watched as Papa threw lengths of strong rope over an impossibly high branch of the tree. He then looped the rope through each handle in turn, creating strong knots to hold the swing steady and level. Once he was satisfied that the swing was secure, he got out his Super Glue.

"Super Glue will hold anything, but you have to be careful, or you'll glue yourself stuck. I built a swing near 'bout as strong as this one for my neighbor's granddaughter. I wasn't careful with the glue and lost my dad-nabbed finger." Papa held up his right hand and showed the stub that was left of his pointer finger. Debbie giggled. She'd heard a hundred different stories of how Papa's finger got lost. She always expected a new one whenever they were together. She had no idea what scary thing had taken Papa's finger, but she had a feeling the truth was not near as fun.

"Yep, there's my fingertip just a swingin' along with Neighbor Hugh's grandbaby for all it's worth. Why, I hear tell she uses it to pick at her nose when she thinks nobody's a-watchin' her." Papa never even cracked a smile. He told every finger story as the Gospel. This one even got Mommy to sniggering behind her hand as she supervised Papa's handiwork.

Papa spread glue liberally in the crannies of the knots and then ran a bead of it around spots where the handles met the seat, just like he did when he caulked Granny's bathtub every winter. Once he got that done, he held the swing upside down and glued the bolts. Next, he got out his other favorite product, petroleum jelly. He made a fist that left his stub sticking out and got him a dip of the jelly and proceeded to rub it on his lips.

"I sure am glad I've got me this here stub. Did you know it cures chapped lips?" Papa asked.

"Oh, Daddy, you just go on and on," Mommy groaned.

"Why, I can recall repairing your chapped lips with this slicked up stub when you weren't much bigger than Debbie. You even asked for a stub from Santy Claus just so you wouldn't have to walk around with your lips all chapped and looking ugly as pootin' in church."

"I want a stub, too!" Debbie chimed in, grinning.

"Now, as convenient as this here stub is, what for applying my jelly and all, I want you to keep all your pretty little fingers.

You might have a mind to pick at your own nose, and a stub's just no good for that."

"Daddy!" Mommy sounded just like a little girl.

Papa was on a roll now and couldn't stop himself. His mouth was just as serious as could be, but his eyes were laughing. Debbie knew what was coming up next, and so did Mommy, who turned on her heel, muttering something about manners and making sweet tea. Papa just rolled on without even hesitating to watch her into the house.

"Debbie, did you know that this stub is a trumpet tooter? Go ahead, give it a little pull, and it'll play for you." Debbie barely touched Papa's hand before he broke wind with a rattling blast, and they both erupted in laughter.

Papa took some more of the petroleum jelly, this time in the palm of his hand, and set to working it into the rope around where Debbie would hold on as she swung.

"Whatcha doing that for, Papa? The swing ain't got lips."

"No, but this rope might have teeth. I'm softening it up so it'll glide smooth in your hands." He worked the jelly into the rope for a good long time. Debbie was about to give up on ever getting to try out the swing when Papa said, "One last step, Debbie, and I'll let you take it for a test drive."

"What's that, Papa? It looks ready to me," she replied, fairly jumping with anticipation.

"Run to the kitchen, and get your Papa a glass of tea, and then I'll be ready to give you a push."

Debbie was off like a March hare and came back not just with the tea, but with Mommy toting the baby, too. For a change, Brent wasn't squalling. Papa had set the swing high enough for Debbie to have to give a little leap to seat herself. She faced the smelly sage, and before she knew it, her feet were flying up into the sky. She squealed in delight as Papa pushed her higher and higher. After all too short a time, Papa brought the swing to a halt and hopped her off the seat.

"What you've got yourself here, Debbie, is a deluxe two-way, self-service swing, guaranteed to make you fly whenever you have a mind to."

He sat her back down on the swing…only this time she was facing Papa and the house. He taught her how to pump her legs to get the swing swinging. Once she got the hang of it, she could almost reach the green of the giant oak. She laughed as the wind rushed through her hair, and she watched her feet rise, flying, hanging for a long second, and then suspended, rushing backward, swooping low before rising again. It was in the height of her reverse arc that she noticed the mountain standing beyond the yard. The mountain has eyes.

The thought came as suddenly and as unbidden as a voice. Her bare arms and legs erupted in goose pimples. Mommy, Papa, and even Baby Brent were grinning like fools as she slid by them, but the joy of the moment was gone. The mountain loomed between her feet, barreling closer and closer. Terrified, Debbie catapulted herself from the swing.

"No!" shouted Papa as she hurtled toward the back porch steps, gaining altitude. For a brief moment, the mountain came toward her. Then she lost sight of it as gravity did its work. Papa was backpedaling, trying to break her fall, trying to catch her like one of Bear Bryant's receivers would catch a pass. He sprung in a last-ditch burst of will. He brushed her with his fingertips as they both fell. But it was enough. The force of Papa's hands altered her course. Her right arm snapped as she met the hard-packed ground inches away from the back steps and crumpled in a heap.

Papa's head thumped as it struck the corner of the bottom step and split open. The impact caused his head to bounce. Everything moved in slow motion, like the instant replays Daddy watched on TV. Before his head came back to rest, a wood-specked spatter of red and milky gray caught the sunlight. Mommy was screeching. Her tea glass shattered as she dashed it to the ground, running to Papa. Debbie watched the tea seep into the dirt. Brent was squalling again. Something else was on the ground. Papa's false teeth lay glistening, tinged with blood. Her arm was throbbing, broken. Papa turned toward Debbie with drowned eyes.

"Damn stub," he muttered…and was gone.

Time fell back into its rhythm. Mommy was cradling Papa's bloody head in her arms, crying "Daddy! Daddy!" Brent was wriggling on the grass in a full-out screaming fit. Mommy lifted her head to Heaven and started screaming, outmatching Baby Brent with a wretchedness that only comes when a heart is wrenched. Debbie whimpered, dazed from her fall, and crazy with the pain in her arm.

Daddy burst through the back door, the sounds of a TV football game following him. "What the hell's all this racket about? Debbie? Caro?" He saw Mommy cradling Papa and both his children on the ground. All of them were howling, save Papa, whose eyes stared blankly at Debbie, the mountain reflecting in his sightless eyes.

"Tell me he's not dead!" shouted Mommy, shaking uncontrollably, as Papa's gray matter oozed into her lap. She knew the truth. Daddy knew the truth. Debbie knew the truth.

"Come away, Caro."

"No! I won't let him go!"

"Carolyn Clemm, come away." He called her first and middle names just like he did whenever Debbie was in trouble. "The baby's crying. Debbie's hurt."

"It's her fault. She killed him. She killed my daddy." Mommy whispered it, but Debbie heard just the same. As soon as the venom came out of her mouth, Mommy started howling again. "Baby, I didn't mean it. I didn't mean it. Oh, my daddy's dead!"

Daddy picked up Brent as Debbie scooted back against the oak tree, her arm hanging limply. He left Mommy holding Papa's body and went back inside. He didn't come back out until Debbie heard the wail of the ambulance siren. It was just minutes later, but it seemed like hours had passed. Two men in uniform followed Daddy, and they were chatting about the football game as if nothing bad had happened at all.

It took a sedative to pry Mommy from Papa. The paramedics pronounced Papa to be dead, which was obvious, and loaded him into the ambulance. They offered to put Debbie in the ambulance, too, but Daddy refused. He'd bring her along to the emergency room once he got Mommy and the baby settled. "After all," Daddy said, "it weren't nothing but a broke arm, and kids've been breaking arms ever since there were kids."

It was cool and dark. Debbie was inside the crook of her oak, but she didn't remember crawling in there. Daddy's face appeared, his voice gentle. "Debbie, come on out. We need to go get your arm fixed up. It's going to be okay. You're going to be okay." He walked her around the side yard, where she wasn't allowed to play, toward the front of the house. GodLutherYouStink followed them with his eyes from his burrow up under the house but didn't bother to wriggle out and investigate.

Daddy avoided the back steps as he walked Debbie and shielded her from seeing them, but she knew she would never unsee them. The paramedics had hosed them down. They had washed Papa's bits of blood and brain off the steps and into the soil. They had picked up the broken glass and the broken teeth. The swing hung dead still, not even a breeze coaxing it to motion. It would be a long time, maybe never, before she would sit in it again.

It wasn't her fault. It was the mountain's fault. She skittered up against the house, trying to use Daddy as a shield between her and the mountain. The mountain stood silent as they passed.

The sheriff's deputy came by the next day. This time, he came into the house, all low-voiced and apologetic. He sat down on the couch beside Debbie, her arm in a sling, and asked her to explain how the accident happened.

"Am I going to go to jail?" Debbie asked just above a hush. She was muddle-headed from the pain medicine the nurse gave her as they set her arm. Mommy and Brent were asleep in the bedroom. She hadn't seen them since it happened. She guessed they'd given Brent a sedative, too, even though he was just a baby and didn't know anything anyhow.

"Of course not, honey," the deputy intoned. "When somebody dies...er...passes on, we just write down the story of how it happened. Can you remember what happened?"

Debbie sighed. "I was swinging extra high, and the mountain scared me. I jumped out of the swing. Papa tried to catch me, but he fell and hit his head."

The deputy shifted uncomfortably on the couch and looked over at Daddy, who was standing in front of the TV with his arms folded. Debbie could tell that Daddy didn't like the deputy. She didn't think the deputy lost any love over her daddy, either. "That's the right of it. She was swinging too high and bailed off. Her granddaddy was trying to catch her."

"Where were you when this happened, Mr. Ballard?"

"I was here in the house watching the game, of course," Daddy replied coolly.

"Thank you, little lady," the deputy said to Debbie as he shook her good hand. "That should be all we'll need." He stood to go. Daddy strode to the front door to see him out. The deputy was a good head taller than Daddy. Tall men made Daddy mad just to look at them. The deputy turned just as he got to the door and addressed Debbie one more time. "Ain't no count bein' afraid of a mountain. It's stuck in its place. Nothin' moves but the shadows. Remember that, now, and let that arm heal up."

Daddy stepped the deputy out on the porch, but the deputy wasn't quite ready to leave. He stood over Daddy and shook his head. "Those back steps are hell on old men, Ballard. Old Man Abby slipped durin' that big ice storm winter 'fore last and went pretty much the same way as your daddy-in-law. You might ought to consider puttin' in some safer steps."

"I don't think the steps have anything to do with it. Besides, I'm just renting this house. There's no call to do home improvements on what ain't yours to start with. I'm sure you have other business, deputy."

"Yes, I do. Tell your wife I'm sorry for her loss, Ballard. And I reckon I agree with you."

"'Bout what?"

"I don't think them steps have anything to do with it, either."

3

Summer crept on toward the start of school with a barely breathable humidity that even made the maple leaves curl in on themselves, as if saving their strength for the molten goldenrods, amethysts, and deep rubicund hues the trees would paint themselves in October. The clove of the season, where summer spent itself unapologetically, plodded on like the schoolchildren Debbie had read about, creeping unwillingly to school. But Debbie felt differently. She could not wait to walk down the first grade hall of the Caldwell Elementary School with her new satchel in hand. First, though, she had to outlast the heat, outlast Brent's incessant squalling, and outlast the menacing presence of Fat Sarah.

There had been some reprieve from Fat Sarah's caretaking during the week after Papa's funeral, but Mommy had to go back to work, and once again, Fat Sarah was fetched to care for the children of the little, green house. Debbie was wary as she watched the babysitter prepare a hearty breakfast of scrambled eggs, canned biscuits, and a salty ham slice and sit down to eat while Debbie's cold bowl of oatmeal congealed at the table. Fat Sarah didn't say a word but looked sharply at Debbie as she sawed into her ham. Her hand went to her pocket, and out came a chocolate bar which she laid on the table, sliding it directly across to Debbie. Her eyes bore into Debbie, and the girl shrank as she realized what Fat Sarah was saying without even opening her mouth, except to shovel in her scrambled eggs. Debbie's hand closed around the candy bar, knowing full well she was making a pact. She slunk from the table and headed for the back door.

Debbie hesitated at the stoop. There was no longer any trace of Papa's blood that had trickled across the uneven surface of the wooden step. Nothing was left of Papa except a lifeless body buried deep in the ground at the cemetery near his house. Debbie had been curious about the hole surrounding Papa's casket. The funeral attendants had covered the area with an ugly green carpet that was supposed to look like grass, but the color was all wrong. His casket stood under a tent, and the carpet grass wasn't smoothed out. Debbie had been afraid she might trip as she had to walk up to the casket to take one of the roses that she was supposed to give to Mommy. She thought that was a bad payout. Mommy lost her father, and all she got from the funeral was a brochure with a sad poem printed on it and a rose that would die just like her grandfather had.

What if she fell, too? The steps were rough-hewn, though worn smooth in the footpath. But for a gash on the bottom rung, the steps appeared just like they always had. The gash wasn't much of a gash, just a place where some wood had been stripped away, about an inch long. It marked the spot where Papa's head made impact. Did Papa feel that splinter go into his head?

"Go on, girl. Your grandpa ain't haunting them steps." Fat Sarah motioned with her ham knife. "Why, you could even swing awhile if you have a mind to. Don't be expectin' me to come out and catch you if you bail out again." Fat Sarah made a sound that could have been a chuckle, or maybe she just had a hunk of ham go down the wrong way.

The morning promised to be a muggy one, with the air still and thick. Debbie hopped over the last step, Papa's step, even though the jarring of the hop made her broken arm twinge. She scurried for the solace of her oak where she could be hidden from the eyes of Fat Sarah and the eyes of July Mountain. After sitting a few minutes with her back snug against the wall of the

21

cool, woody hollow, she noticed the swing. It hung so sorrowfully in its tree. She knew Mommy would never let her swing again or put Baby Brent on it when he got big enough to sit and swing. It was like fun that had been ruined by a sudden storm. It was like coloring a pretty picture and then scribbling over it. The picture was still there, underneath, but it was messed up and no longer had its appeal. It needed to be wadded up and thrown away, but how can a memory be thrown away? If she was to swing again, would she be able to feel the air flowing through her hair? Could she swing without smelling death?

Debbie sighed as she looked at the limpid swing and was sorry she'd recalled the smell. That was part of what had frightened her so much. The moment she had felt the eyes of the mountain upon her, she had caught scent, a scent so real and rank and out of place that it had terrified her. That final arc of the swing stopped time. The mountain yawed. It spoke those words: The mountain has eyes. It breathed its insidious breath toward the little, green house sitting in its shadow, under its fist. She had swung through the smell, acrid and cloying, sweet rot, barreling upward and upward, closer and closer to the mountain. It opened its mouth, and Debbie jumped.

That's what Debbie remembered, and that's the secret Debbie told to her tree because even though she was only five years old, she was old enough to know that no grownup could ever understand. She was old enough to know that mountains don't move. They don't breathe. They don't speak, but she had the truth of it. She had the sentience of experience. She had seen. She had heard. She had smelled. She had tasted. Her fear had been palpable. Debbie knew the mountain was about to claim someone. It wanted her. It wanted to swallow her up, but she had jumped, and it took Papa instead.

Debbie had felt the shadow of Death and careened through it, air bound, if but for a moment. And in that moment, she had

22

recognized the terror of not knowing for whom it had come. In that moment, she was not a little girl at all.

She focused on the swing again, trying to look at it as a plaything. She felt some better...now that her secret was out. The tree enveloped her in silence, which she took for its understanding and assent. The morning was so still that the air was stifling even in the shade of the tree's cranny. She scrunched around and up on her knees so that she could reach the hole she had found inside her tree. The wood was soft and pliable around the hole, and she began to work it with her fingers. She only thought about spiders once, but her trust in the tree was enough that she felt it wouldn't "let" a spider bite her. It smelled earthy, loamy, as she tried to peer into the hole. The smell was fertile, like the ground right after Daddy had tilled it so Mommy could plant her tomatoes. It made Debbie feel hopeful. Rotted wood fell away, and the hole expanded. She could've opened it more if not for the cast, but she had enough room to do what she intended to do anyway, so it didn't really matter. Debbie reached into her pocket and pulled out the candy bar Fat Sarah had made her take. "I wish Fat Sarah would go away," she whispered into the heart of the tree. She deposited the candy bar into the hole, knowing she'd never really take candy from Fat Sarah again.

Debbie sat back down, pleased with herself. She was pleased with the pact she'd made with the oak tree. The oak would teach her how to stand tall against the monsters, whether they be thieving babysitters, mountains, or death itself. Candy bars and swings were supposed to be treats, playthings for little girls to enjoy. She would make sure that Baby Brent would not have his child-right fun stolen away. She would make sure he stayed safe because she knew she would never forget that smell. If she ever smelled it again, she would protect her baby brother, even though he cried most of the time.

As she stood to head back into the house for lunchtime, the swing began to move. She looked up into the trees, grateful for a bit of breeze, but the leaves were dead still. There was no breeze at all. The swing drew forward, ever so slightly, as if an invisible hand were pulling it up, before releasing it to totter back and forth. It was enough. The mountain had been watching.

4

First grade was the best thing that had ever happened to Debbie. She got to spend the entire day learning new things, and her teacher, Mrs. Williams, allowed her to read from the third grade section of the library. Best of all was Playground Day. Once a week, Mrs. Williams walked the class to the wooded playground just across the street from the school. There were three merry-go-rounds! The smallest was painted bright yellow and spun dizzyingly fast. It would be the scene of another broken arm the last day of fourth grade, but for now, Debbie was out of her cast, fully healed from the summer accident. The medium merry-go-round was set on an angle and allowed children to sit on benches and dangle their legs as they spun. The large merry-go-round was the slowest, but the entire class could ride at once, the boys clamoring to be chosen to push.

Debbie's absolute favorite part of playground time, though, was swinging. Here, she could soar without worrying about the mountain, without worrying about the memories. The shade trees hid her line of vision, and she knew that if she couldn't see the mountain, it couldn't see her. Here, Mommy couldn't make her sad face as Debbie grinned at the tickling in her tummy. Here, she did not have to hide in her tree.

Still, Debbie had the afternoon hours to endure with Fat Sarah before Daddy returned from work. Mommy was a nurse at the hospital and worked from three in the afternoon until eleven o'clock each weeknight. This meant that Debbie only saw her for a few minutes each morning before the school bus picked her up. Debbie would be fast asleep before Mommy returned. Debbie had a hard time being comfortable around Mommy since Papa died. Sometimes, she would catch Mommy staring at her with such an intense sadness that Debbie could hardly bear it. Blame hid just behind the sadness. Mommy tried to conceal it, but it seeped out anyway, slipping down her face alongside her tears for Papa.

As the school bus approached the little, green house each afternoon, Debbie would become more subdued. At school, she was free. At home, she was afraid. Fat Sarah would always be standing at the door and would usher Debbie immediately to the kitchen table where a plate of milk and cookies would await, along with the expected chocolate bar. On the surface, everything appeared to be perfectly normal. A first grader would get home from school and enjoy a snack, but appearances can be deceiving, and sometimes a six year old has an uncannily accurate perception of what lies beneath a benign surface.

Fat Sarah held Baby Brent on her hip as she waddled about the kitchen preparing supper. He had started to whimper and was getting himself warmed up for an all-out crying jag, but Fat Sarah jiggled him up and down on her hip. He was not yet big enough to walk but was growing quickly.

"Why, look-a-here, Brent. You've done gotten too big for my roasting pan," she cooed in a singsong voice that made the baby settle almost immediately. "You're just as sweet as sugar, baby, baby. Why, I could just eat you up." Her voice was all honey, but her words had a sinister ring. Debbie could imagine her trying to put the baby in the oven just like the witch did in the story of Hansel and Gretel that Mrs. Williams told during Heads-Down Time, the only part of the school day Debbie could do without.

Saying and meaning were two different things. Even with stories at school, what Mrs. Williams told was only a part of what a story meant. It was the same with grownups who weren't

26

teachers. Fat Sarah, Daddy, Mommy, and even the sheriff's deputy talked with way more than their words. Debbie could watch, and Debbie could listen. And when she sat in her tree and remembered their words, Debbie could understand what they meant, what they wanted to say, and what they didn't want to say. It was a lot like reading, only with people instead of pages. Problem was sometimes she knew more than a little girl should. She just had to figure out which layers to show and which layers to squirrel away in the hollows. A chocolate bar could be just as sweet uneaten, and too much deliciousness could be just as yucky as a helping of lima beans. Debbie let these thoughts melt into her as she whiled away the interval before Daddy arrived to whisk Fat Sarah back to her own life, which Debbie didn't care to know a thing about.

5

"A cloud's coming up; could be a bad one," Fat Sarah announced from the stove, where she was fixing a beef stew. Daddy wasn't due home for another two hours or so, and dark was coming on fast. "Little Debbie, if you're going to go talk to that tree of yours, you'd best head on out before it starts up raining again. You might want to ask it to protect you tonight. It's looking bad out, and I'll be gone on home by then. I'd hate for a storm to get you and this here little baby." She looked into the beef stew as she talked, like she was divining the future.

Gusts of wind swirled the limbs of the trees, and the trunks of the smaller ones swayed to the rhythm of the breeze, their leaves whispering urgently. The trees were sharing some secret news that was being passed from limb to limb, some news that came from the mountain, or perhaps beyond. The air was thick even with the wind trying to stir it. It was too warm for the rain jacket Fat Sarah had given her, so Debbie just hooked the hood on her head as she descended the steps into the yard. Even now, she carefully avoided Papa's step, but the memory of the ordeal had faded, much as it tends to do in children.

It takes a lot to destroy a child, but not so very much to plant the seeds of destruction. A child can nurture those seeds with wishes and tears. A child will coddle those base desires and color them in until she mistakes the very beast she's created for hope. Deep down, childlike innocence is neither childlike nor innocent.

"You forgot your candy," Fat Sarah called from the back door. She glanced up at the sky, shook her head, and tossed the bar down to Debbie. As she turned to go back into the house, her eyes turned to the mountain. "Faith can move a mountain, but one day, the mountain shall fall," she said to nobody in particular. The screen door whacked shut behind her.

The oaken nook protected Debbie from both the wind and the rain, but the ground inside was damp. She put down her raincoat as a tarp and reached up into the heart of the tree to work the hollow. She expanded the opening a little bit each day, rubbing and pushing handfuls of soft wood, almost gone to sawdust, down into the depths of the tree. She fed the tree her chocolate bars and whispered Fat Sarah's name into the hollow. The tree, in return, offered her its silent protection, and, maybe before long, it would also offer her the most perfect of hiding places. She could have a nook within her nook if she needed to squirrel herself away. Fat Sarah wouldn't be able to see her hiding place, much less fit in to get at her, and surrounded by oak, Debbie felt the eyes of the mountain could not reach her because she would be out of bounds.

But that's the problem with mountains. They don't play by a child's rules. A girl can carve out a safe haven one spoonful at a time, and it won't make any difference at all to the mountain.

Although the tree was silent in terms of language, Debbie had spent enough time in her hollow to know that a tree is a living thing. It has knowledge and wisdom. A tree can talk, if a person has the ears to hear it. Sitting still as a stone, Debbie could listen to the tree. She could feel the faint vibrations against the trunk as the branches caught breezes, clacking their twigs together and pretending to sail. That's what Debbie thought her oak longed to do. She just knew that its greatest wish was to fly, to sail on clouds, to move from the spot it was rooted. She and the tree were a lot alike. Her tree wanted to escape the shadow of the mountain just as much as she did. But

29

her tree had withstood its gaze ever so much longer than she had, and for that, Debbie loved her tree.

Debbie always seemed to lose track of time when sitting inside her tree. She must have been napping, the pitter of raindrops on the grass a lullaby, but something had jarred her awake. Had the tree just shuddered? There was a tremble in the ground, almost imperceptible. Suddenly, Fat Sarah's face loomed in the entrance of the cranny.

"Debbie!" she screeched, "Get out of there, now!"

"What is it?" Debbie was suddenly terrified. She scrabbled out from the tree into a melee of noise, swirling leaves, and her screaming baby brother. GodLutherYouStink was making strange noises caught somewhere between a bark, a howl, and a whimper. Something was wrong with the color outside. Something was wrong with the air. It suddenly became hard to breathe, and Debbie's ears popped. She felt like she was falling. The sky was green, almost as green as the house. The rain started in earnest, and Debbie turned back to the tree to retrieve her raincoat.

"Girl! There's no time for that! Come on!" Fat Sarah stood out in the yard, holding onto Brent way too tightly. She stared at the mountain with her mouth agape. "It comes! The mountain moves! I have the baby! I have the baby!" Madness was in her eyes. What was Fat Sarah doing? Debbie could not tell if her screams were a defense or an offering. Time shifted into slow motion as Debbie's senses went into hyper-sensation. A downdraft brought with it an acrid smell, part electricity, part rot. Debbie recognized the smell instantly, instinct triggering memory that plumbed fathoms deeper than childhood experience. The Saint Bernard knew, too, working furiously on the chain.

The rain blew sideways, soaking Debbie, Fat Sarah, and the baby alike. The wind roared down the mountain. Fat Sarah staggered against it, trying to get to the safety of the house, but it pushed her backwards toward the tree with Papa's swing. She still gripped the baby, shielding him against leaves and limbs that peppered the back yard in the fury of the wind. Debbie was on her knees, crawling toward Fat Sarah. As sudden as the fury of weather had begun, it stopped. In that moment of silence, the air stank of death. The trees stood up, the rain ceased to fall, and everything held its breath, a sharp intake of nature attempting to prepare itself for what was to come.

"Get inside! Get inside!" yelled Fat Sarah, even though she was standing planted to the ground. Brent wailed, but his cries were drowned out by another sound unlike any Debbie had ever heard. Fat Sarah pointed toward the sound. Debbie turned, too. The light shifted from peevish green to gray-black in an instant. The storm wall swallowed the mountain, an ugly witch's finger reaching down from the sky to trace the curves of the mountainside. And the mountain roared. It started as a howl, wind run amok, but developed into a deafening thunder, like the sound of a train engine motoring through a tunnel. The sound swallowed everything. Debbie's hands clapped over her ears, which continued to pop as if the wind was trying to suck the air up out of her body. Trees tumbled down the mountainside, scattering as if they were nothing but twigs. The funnel cloud pushed the mountain closer. The mountain was moving, moving toward her, moving toward Fat Sarah, and moving toward Brent. The smell of rot clung to her like the wet leaves battering against her face as she watched, helpless, in the path of the storm, in the path of the mountain's wrath.

Debbie was terrified. The maelstrom was bearing down upon them all, and Fat Sarah was standing there screaming, but steadfast.

"Crawl under the house!" she shouted at Debbie, but Debbie remained frozen, partially in fear and partially in recognition. "Crawl under the house, or the mountain will take you, too!" Fat Sarah's screams were derisive. Limbs, debris, and inexplicably, a mailbox scudded across the back yard. A chicken, dispossessed of most of its feathers flew headlong into

31

the trunk of the great oak, airborne on an unnatural flight that ended in a lifeless heap at the base of the tree.

"No!" shouted Debbie. "Give me Brent!" Debbie was on hands and knees, trying to get beneath the wind, which fought to separate her from her baby brother, but didn't seem to affect Fat Sarah at all. The wind had ripped the bun from Fat Sarah's head, and her hair, a mixture of gray and brown, whipped around her head in snake-like coils. Debbie was pelted with leaves, twigs, and a few good-sized limbs as she crawled her way ever so slowly toward her squalling baby brother. She could hear the train roaring behind her but was afraid to look back over her shoulder. She knew she had to get to Brent, had to get him out of the clutches of Fat Sarah, who had begun to laugh. Fat Sarah's laugh was almost as frightening as the noise of the storm. She had now lifted Brent high over her head, offering him to the storm, or to the mountain, or to whatever monster was chewing up the land in its path.

"No!" Debbie screamed again. "You can't have him!" Whether she was rebelling against Fat Sarah, the storm, or the mountain itself was unclear, but the force of her will made something happen. Papa's swing careened wildly in the storm. It fluttered overhead like a kite in the March breeze. She wanted it to hit Fat Sarah. She wanted it to hurt Fat Sarah. She wanted to save her baby brother more than anything. "Help me!" she screamed. She was almost crazy herself with fear.

There was a crunch as the limb holding the swing split from the tree. The wind swirled so much it was hard to tell, but the limb rose rather than fell, setting the swing into an arc that for the briefest second, flew into the face of the storm. The winds regained their hold, and the swing barreled toward Fat Sarah so quickly she didn't have time to react. It slammed into her, trailing the detached limb, catching her just under the chin, and severing her windpipe on impact. Debbie watched Papa's swing continue to rise on the wings of the storm as Fat Sarah crumpled, knees buckling beneath her heft, dead before she hit

32

the ground. The force of the swing had loosed Fat Sarah's grip on Brent. He seemed to hang in the air as the ropes sliced to either side of his rain-soaked blanket. Fat Sarah's lifeless body broke his fall. He tumbled gently off her stomach and rolled toward Debbie, wailing all the while.

Debbie sprang from her crouch, snatching the baby away from the danger of Fat Sarah. She snuggled him to her and turned to face the storm. The tips of the pine trees skirting the field across the road pointed toward her, bent sideways as the funnel cloud finished its descent down the mountainside and dug into the ground. Their trunks snapped like giant firecrackers in the force of the wind.

Bring him to me, quickly. The oak limbs swept the ground in the wind, blocking any route of escape but itself. Debbie obeyed her tree. She scurried into the cranny, almost squashing the baby as she fell against the wall of trunk. What had always seemed a world inside the embrace of the tree now seemed miniscule in the face of the fury trucking toward them. She might not save herself, but she could save Brent. She scrabbled desperately at the hole where she had secreted away the ugly promises of those chocolate bars and the even uglier wishes of her heart. It would be tight, but it would do. She could squirrel him away and hide him from the mountain storm. He'd be safe in the heart of the oak.

It took all her strength to lift the baby into the scrabbled hole. She knew he would fall but hoped the tree's roots would bolster him. She kissed him square on the lips and whispered her prayer or her wish. Did it really matter which one it was? Her last wish had freed Brent from certain death. Perhaps she had the power to do it again.

"I've got you, baby," she said as she got ready to release him into the depth of the oak.

The baby stopped crying and said, "Deb."

She let him drop.

The tree trembled and shook. Debbie made herself as small as possible inside the hollow of the oak. The noise was deafening. The tree stood, sheltering them from the madness just outside its girth. The wind screamed—or maybe she was screaming—glass shattered, and wood splintered. She could no longer hear the dog. The tree gave a lurch as its roots let go, no longer able to hold against the force of the storm. She became a roly-poly, a tiny ball as the tree toppled around her, on top of her. Debbie reached upward for a purchase, for protection, latching onto the rim of the hole in which she'd sent her baby brother. Either the strength of her terror or the weight of the toppling tree made the softened wood give way. She felt something wriggle at her feet. A small hand grasped her scraped and bloodied ankle as her mouth filled with the loam of a worm-eaten tree, not much more than a shell. Blackness engulfed them, swallowed, but not crushed. Even the sound of the storm was muffled when the tree fell upon them, sacrificing itself in one last act of defense.

The darkness was disorienting, but it gave Debbie what comfort it could. She couldn't see Brent, but she could feel him. Somehow he'd been cradled between her rear end and backs of her legs. He sneezed twice and settled into the rhythmic breathing of sleep. She was glad he wasn't crying. Not hearing his cries made her realize something else: silence.

The storm had passed at last. Her tree had saved them both. She let the silence wash over her, and her tears flowed. She cried for what she had lost in the storm, and she cried for what she had gained. Her beloved tree was downed, but her baby brother was safe and sound. It did not occur to her that they were trapped, and she felt no fear. Time passed, trailing the storm, as she rested in the embrace of the tree. She had learned how a mountain can move, how it can fling its trees like missiles at children if it so chooses.

Her mind raced with questions trying to process what had happened, trying to find a sense of order, or at least an earthy logic. Did Fat Sarah call down the storm? Did the mountain draw down its wrath, like a giant magnet, and send it raging toward them?

All she knew for certain was that Fat Sarah would never speak her frightening words all coated in sugary chocolate, sweet and smooth, but ugly on the inside, ever again. She knew that when she gave Baby Brent back, Mommy would love her once again. Papa had died, but Brent was saved. The storm, as terrifying as it was, had freed her from the grip of fears known and unknown.

***

The sunset that evening was spectacular, as sunsets tend to be once the sky has cleansed itself with a storm. The air blew cool, the promise of winter on its breath. The light streamed pinks and reds down over the mountain, scarred and ugly, over a swath of destruction. People emerged from their storm shelters, closets, and out from under their porches, blinking first into the late afternoon splendor and then hanging their heads as they looked at the chaos around them.

Sirens wailed, and people prayed for thanksgiving, deliverance, or comfort as was their lot. Neighbors, some who hadn't spoken to each other for years beyond a "How are you?" at the mailbox, stood together to assess the damage and to take census. They counted their kin and moved the search circle outward.

When a tornado touches down, digging up ground, tossing trees, cars, and even houses as if they were a child's playthings in a sandbox, people tend to come together. It's the randomness of the storm. Folks want to assign meaning to it, where really there's none. The tornado will decimate one home and leave the one right next to it untouched. Reason has as little to do with the path of the storm as luck. Nature is the greatest equalizer of all. There's no difference between young and old, rich and poor, shouting Baptists and Whiskey-palians. All quail; all tremble. Some live; some die. Some do a little of both.

It's the illogicalness of the tornado that is terrifying. Preachers will preach on secret sin and on the hand of God, but the tornado knows no difference between the sacred and the profane. It's just as likely to blow a church to smithereens as it is a brothel. It may leave nothing but a hall closet standing in a house, with a grown man whimpering quietly inside, shaken, but none the worse for the wear. It may take a grandmother huddling over her grandbabies in a bathtub, bathing them in prayer that wasn't enough to save her as well.

It jumps and skips across the area it possesses, leaving a litter of curious souvenirs of its destructive power. A car may be crushed like an empty beer can, tangled in the roof of a house a hundred yards away from where a couple of randy teenagers were necking, the windshield and their brains too fogged to register what was coming for them. A single strand of hay may pierce a telephone pole like a dart quivering in a bull's-eye. A pair of children may emerge unscathed from the exposed root system of a fallen oak tree.

6

"It's the damnedest thing I've ever seen," Deputy Barnevelder shook his head as he stood in the upturned earth, the roots of the oak rising head high. "I can't make sense of how them children survived it nor why on earth they'd try to shelter there instead of somewhere in or up under the house, but I'm sure glad they did. You're a damn lucky man, Ballard."

"Lucky in that, but not so lucky elsewhere. Damn storm took half my house, and my dog's laying dead out in the yard," Daddy replied. "It wasn't much of a house, but we're gonna have to find somewhere else to stay. Hell, it wasn't much of a dog, either, to tell the truth of it. Damn thing stunk to high heaven."

Papa's steps were still intact but led up into nothing. The kitchen was simply gone. The living room couch had slid off in the hole that used to be the kitchen. It looked like somebody had taken a giant butcher knife to the back end of the house, chopped it off, and swept the leavings away. The front of the house wobbled on its pilings, and, but for a slight list to the east, where the wind had pushed it, appeared unharmed. The glass in the windows wasn't blown out, but the pressure drop as the tornado struck had shredded the curtains. They hung lifeless and ruined.

Mommy was sitting in her nurse's cap and uniform on Papa's steps, her back to the broken house, a litter of green siding at her feet. She held Brent in one arm like she would never let go and had her other arm tight around Debbie, tears streaming shamelessly down her face. She had left her post at the hospital to race home as soon as she heard the storm barreled off July Mountain and into Woods Cove.

"I thought I was going to lose you both," she repeated, rocking and hugging. Both of them were dirty as pigs from crawling through the rain-soaked roots, and Mommy's white uniform was mud-splattered, but she didn't seem to mind. Brent had taken up crying again from exhaustion and the need for a bottle that had flown to who-knows-where.

"I don't understand why Fat, er, Sarah would've had the babies outside in all this," Daddy turned back to the deputy. "I sure hope she wasn't in the kitchen."

"I'll call in the rescue squad, and we'll start a search. It'll be dark all too soon. It's going to be cold tonight. It's like to start raining again, too. I'd hate for her to be hurt and us not able to find her till tomorrow. She can't be far."

"Sarah!" Daddy shouted. "Sarah, where are you?"

"Mr. Ballard, let me look for Sarah. She's distant kin, anyway. You need to look to your family. We'll find her," Deputy Barnevelder instructed.

"She isn't lost," Debbie said as she pointed to the tangle of limbs from the fallen oak, "She's in there, killed."

"Dammit. I'm going to need a chainsaw to get her out of there. Are you sure, Little Debbie?"

"Yes, sir. Papa's swing got her first, and then my tree squashed her. And from now on, I'm not Little Debbie. That's what she called me, and I hate it. I hate her. She won't be hurting me or Brent ever again. I'm Deb." The words flew from her mouth in a torrent of emotion.

"What are you talking about? Sarah keeps you like you was her own baby. She loves you," Mommy chastised. "That woman has never laid a finger on you although you probably deserved a good spanking on more than one occasion. Sarah loves us all."

38

"That's a lie!" Deb shot back. "She cooked up all our good food and hogged it for herself while she gave me cheese sandwiches. She told me I couldn't tell on her, or she'd hurt the baby. She stole things, too. She was mean! She—"

"Enough! I won't have you talking all this rot when she might be laying out hurt right here in the yard. Now, hush up, Deb, before I give you something to cry about." Daddy drew up his hand.

"Ballard, there's no cause for that. The girl's wrought up is all. Hell, she just rode out a damn tornado in the hollow of a tree, for God's sake. Your girl was all but buried alive and came crawling out of what should've been her grave, dragging your baby son behind her." The deputy's hand rested lightly on his service weapon just to remind Daddy who was really in charge here. His voice gentled. "Mrs. Ballard, why don't you take the young-uns and go wait in your husband's car. I expect y'all will be staying in the motel tonight." She rose obediently, turning automatically to walk through the kitchen door before remembering it no longer existed. "This way, ma'am."

Deputy Barnevelder led them around the side of the house, hoping the girl wouldn't get distraught over the heap of dog out by the road. He should've found a tarp or something to throw over it before he brought the family around. He looked up at the mountain, an ugly path clear-cut down its side.

"Little Deb…" He stopped himself before he called her the name she hated. "Look how deep the mountain's cut by the storm, and you able to hide safe inside that tree like a squirrel, keeping your baby brother in your care. You've been a brave girl, but that storm has cut you deep, too…, in here." The deputy pointed to her heart. "But don't you worry. That mountain's gonna heal up and grow back just as pretty and proud as it was before. Why, before long, you won't even be able to see its scar. You see, you're a lot like that mountain. That storm has left a big ole hurt, but your heart will grow over

39

the sore spots, and you'll be able to see things in a different way, with mountain eyes."

She looked up at the mountain. It didn't look scarred to her; it looked chewed. Whether the storm was trying to kill her or save her, she wasn't sure. The one thing she was sure of was that the mountain did have eyes, mean eyes, and she knew she'd had them, too, when she had faced down Fat Sarah. Maybe the deputy was right. Maybe she was like the mountain, but that was hardly a comfort.

"Thank you, Deputy." Daddy had reappeared at their sides, ready to usher them to the car. "I'll put them in the car so you can start moving that tree aside. Honey, y'all wait here for just a minute while I grab the sheets off the bed. I'll throw them on the back seat. We've got enough to clean up as it is without y'all mucking up my car to boot."

The rescue squad wheeled in, and Deb heard a chainsaw fire up before Daddy had time to come back out of the house with the covers.

"I've got to see," said Daddy. "I'll just be a little while, and then I'll drive us to the motel like the deputy said." From the back seat, Deb could just see GodLutherYouStink's tail. The breeze would lift his fur, giving the illusion of a wag. She scrunched herself down in the seat so both the dog and the mountain disappeared, and she closed her eyes.

7

The oak sprawled across the better part of the back yard in a tangled shroud of leaf and limb, many too large for a man to move alone. Its upturned roots, yanked from the ground, were exposed and dangling in a myriad of girths from long, fuzzed tendrils to bracing taproot, strong as a man's thigh. The labyrinthine maze was held together by a mixture of topsoil and clay. It gave the impression of a severed limb, its macerated flesh congealing and acrawl with gangly nerves or worms. It stank of rot.

The deputy stood contemplating the tree, looking for the logic behind the children's survival, but could find none, at least none that could be codified in the lengthy report he had ahead of him. Those kids should be just as dead as that poor old codger who had brained himself when he fell back in the summer. It would take a damn logging crew to get that tree turned so he could investigate the hollow the little girl had squirreled herself and the baby inside. He might try to work his way inside through the exposed roots, but something about that made the hairs on his arm rise. It looked like the roots had coiled in on themselves, grabbing for the soil that clung to them. He'd have to hack his way in like a man cutting through a jungle. There was enough nasty business to attend to in the wake of this storm without trying to explain the physics of what had happened. Besides, he had near about flunked his high school physics class trying to spark Nancy, who sat next to him in class and wound up his wife the Saturday after graduation.

Thinking of Nancy made Barnevelder see the tree in a different light, and he knew he wouldn't be hacking his way inside. That tree had birthed those kids just as sure as Nancy had delivered his son, all pink with blood—his own pumping and Nancy's pushing—gripping the umbilical cord like a tow line as he slid out and bellowed from the ordeal. Other than taking the Lord Jesus Christ as Lord and Savior, he reckoned that the little girl, Debbie, and the baby had been about as born again as folks could be. That baby was too little to harbor any recollection, but it would change the girl. He could feel it in his bones. It had already begun when she proclaimed herself Deb.

"Deputy Barnevelder." A rescue squad man holding a smoking chainsaw shook him from his reverie. "We've found her. You need to have a look at this."

The squad had sawed a pathway through the wreckage. A great pile of limbs was massing, pyre-like against the ruin of another tree on the far border of the yard. That tree looked like the wind had yanked off its upper half and tossed it God-knows where. The deputy saddened. This house would not be a nostalgic old home place in the memory of that little girl. Too much had been lost.

"She's right through here." The worker guided Barnevelder through an obstacle course of limbs twisted every which way but loose, the smell of fresh-cut timber mixing with a distinct odor of rot. "Most of this trunk's rotten, but the limbs are still solid. This tree's seen many a year, much longer than us. That's for sure."

The deputy nodded as the worker, Johnson or maybe it was Jones, prattled on. "It's the damnedest thing I've ever seen."

"So she's dead?" He'd seen enough corpses in his tenure of the law to last a lifetime, mostly car wrecks and a few shootings where some jealous husband or wife had had enough of the other one fooling around.

"Deader than four o'clock. Damn near had her head took off, but that ain't the whole of it," Johnson or Jones replied with a bit of an air about his voice that let Barnevelder know this wasn't his first rodeo with the Reaper either.

Sarah Elder lay dead indeed, her head lolling at an unnatural angle, neck purpled. Her eyes bulged from their sockets as if she were struggling for one last glimpse of life. Her hair streamed out on the ground around her, long and stringy. She had not been easy to look at in life, but in death, she appeared almost beautiful for a woman of her age and girth. But for her head, everything else seemed undisturbed. Her dress covered her body modestly, smoothed down around her legs.

"There wasn't a fallen limb on her. The tree just kind of fell around her," Johnson-Jones said. "I don't get it. She got hit with something, but I don't think it was this tree. I'd best get back to clearing."

"Tornados can do odd things," Barnevelder said equably as he knelt down beside her. Looking up, he noticed the man was right. The fallen tree had missed the spot where she lay. Actually, it canopied the area. The back yard looked like a bomb had exploded, but this spot was clean, or had been cleaned. He had assumed the workers had moved debris off her, but that was not the case. He turned back to Sarah. As he reached to close her eyes, he noticed something else. He hefted her shoulder, being careful of her crushed neck, which appeared to be holding her head on precariously at best. She was a large woman, always had been, so shifting her took some effort. Just under her shoulder was a wrapper, another beside it. He was down on all fours now, perplexed. Just under the drape of Sarah's dress, surrounding her body like a halo, chocolate bars lay end to end. They were not scattered; they were arranged. A tornado destroys half a house and a tree, but candy bars are stacked around the dead babysitter? Oh, Little Debbie, what have you done?

He looked up again. The tree shrouded him from the nearby workers. The chainsaw was whining again. He was utterly alone. Sarah Elder turned her head despite her crushed neck.

43

"Protect her. Protect her. The mountain...eyes," gasped the corpse and then lay dead a second time.

The head fell back into place. He could hear the slosh of liquidy sinew as the neck strained. Her eyes bulged, open and staring, not at him—thank God, not at him—but at the mountain beyond the canopy of the fallen oak. A bubble of blood appeared at the corner of her gaping mouth. Its blue-black surface gave way and began a gelatinous slide onto Sarah's resting jowl.

"Holy Mother of God!" Barnevelder crossed himself even though he hadn't attended Mass since he was a boy visiting his grandmother on summer break. He'd been a good shouting Baptist, washed in the blood of the Lamb for years. That was his wife's doing back in high school. Sitting on her front porch swing with the moon reflecting silver streaks in her hair, she'd looked him in the eye and told him straight up that any boy who didn't know the Lord would have no business knowing her. Then she'd kissed him so long and slow, with such promise in her searching lips and wandering hands, he'd been about set afrenzy. He got saved the next Sunday. It wasn't the Lord's call he was answering at the time, but he hoped that wouldn't make a difference when he one day went knocking on the Pearly Gates.

The gooseflesh crawled on his skin as he quickly gathered the chocolate bars from around Sarah's body. He couldn't imagine what the candy meant other than proof that it wasn't the storm that killed her, but it had to be connected to the girl. He'd at least do this deed. He wanted the dead to stay dead, so he'd help a dead woman out. He sure as hell didn't want a haint on his hands.

It would mean his job if he were caught tampering with evidence. He was on his knees stuffing his shirt with the candy when the wall of the canopy was at last pulled away in a flurry of leaves.

"I didn't count you for the kneeling kind." It was Ballard, Deb's father, a cocky little bastard if ever there was one. It made him feel even more sorry for the girl that she had to put up with this son of a bitch her whole life, or at least until she was grown. Then, maybe, she could get out from under him.

"Just paying my respects," the deputy replied.

"Looks like I'll be searching for a new babysitter as well as a place to live. It's near about impossible to find one that'll cook and clean, too." Ballard was obviously inconvenienced by Sarah's decision to die before consulting him about the matter. "She lived alone. I never heard her talk of any kin, so you saying she's your people is a relief. I was worried I was gonna have to pay for her damn burial. She's gonna need a jumbo-sized casket, and that's sure to be expensive."

"You just take care of yours, Ballard. I'll take of what's mine. Sarah's my aunt, you cheap ass bastard." With that, he brushed past Ballard and left him standing in the ruins.

8

Children have amazing resiliency. When given a bit of time and a change of venue, they can bounce back from adversity with astounding speed. They also have a tendency to weave fact and fiction, happenings and happenstance, into that fabrication called memory. Deb was no different in this aspect. The dual deaths of Papa and Sarah, the tornado, and the miracle of the tree had all knitted together into a one-dimensional corner of her memory under the subheading "Life in the Green House."

Deb rarely even thought of the mountain or Sarah's terrifying threats. They were all gone, clear-cut from her realm of experience in much the same manner the tornado had cut a swath down the side of the mountain. In its place, new life grew.

Of course, over time, the new growth would become non-discernible from the old. Trees grow thick again. Memories and experience intermingle until, without fail, history rears its ugly head and repeats itself. Sins are passed on, generation by generation, daughter to daughter, and time waits with unfathomable patience. It waits for a child to grow; it waits to reveal the next chapter. Time is not linear; it is cyclical. Lives can be intricately connected without being bound by the constraints of a single lifetime.

Deb waited eagerly for the surprise promised by her father. Mommy had taken off work that evening, so the family could enjoy a nice dinner at Scottsboro's only steakhouse. It was certainly exciting for a third grader. Brent was fully embracing his terrible twos, carrying them well into his third year. Really, Deb thought her little brother would never stop shrieking. It was more like braying. Brent's voice was unnaturally low for a toddler, practically baritone. He was the fussiest child Deb could imagine, so much so that she vowed never to have a baby of her own. Brent was fighting against the stays of his highchair, a shower of cracker crumbs falling on the floor around him, and a streak of ketchup across his left cheek. Although he was much too old for it, he drank his chocolate milk from a bottle. This embarrassed Deb, but when he was slugging down his chocolate, he wasn't squalling. That was better for everyone within hearing range.

Brent was now on his fifth babysitter since Fat Sarah. It seemed that the constant crying set even the most patient of caregivers on edge. The latest change had come just a couple of weeks earlier and with no notice. All of their things had been piled in the sitter's driveway, who proclaimed, "Deb is big enough to get on without much watching, but I just can't take your son one moment longer."

Deb was squirmy with excitement, waiting for Daddy to deliver his big news, which he began between bites of bloody steak. He liked to order his steak rare: "Slap its scrawny butt, and send it on to the table," he would say with a smile. He always ordered his steak with a buttery baked potato that he would dissect on the plate, trailing the creamy potato through the beef juices. It created a sickening picture of congealed blood, so much so that Mommy would keep a menu on the table to screen her eyes from Daddy's plate. He cleaned up his steak, gristle and all, and ran his Texas toast across the plate to sop up any remaining liquid. By the time he got finished and pushed his plate to the side, even Mommy was visibly anxious for the news he would share.

"Well, I'd best tell you while Brent's quiet, so I won't have to yell it all over the restaurant," he said. Both Mommy and Deb leaned forward. "I've bought a piece of property. We're building a house!" Deb cheered. She had grown tired of the apartment complex they had lived in since the tornado had taken the back end of the green house.

"You've bought what?" asked Mommy.

"I'm getting us out of the apartment. It's time for the Ballards to move up in the world. We're property owners, Caro."

"You bought a piece of property without even consulting me? Didn't you think I might like to be part of the decision?" Mommy was not smiling. "How can we afford property now? What have you done?"

"I've made a name for us in this one-horse town. That's what I've done. We start construction next week. I've picked you out a fine house, Carolyn. One that you'll be proud to have."

"Didn't you think I might want a say in picking it out? Didn't you think I might want to choose what kind of house we'll build? Didn't you think I might want to have some semblance of a conversation about this before you up and bought something?" Mommy was livid.

"Lower your voice, and show some appreciation. When do you think you could've chosen any of this? You sleep all day and work all night. We're stuck in a rut. You had to take off of work just to come here tonight. The time was right, and the deal was right. I'm trying to make you happy here." Daddy was getting that mean look in his eye, that I-dare-you sort of look that Deb knew meant trouble if Mommy questioned him much beyond where she already had.

Mommy knew the look, too, and cowed down.

"I'm taking you tomorrow morning to see our new lot. We will sign the loan papers Monday and will be in our home by summer. This is a good thing, Caro, and I'm not going to let you spoil it." Daddy had a tone that meant business.

Deb watched the exchange over her junior cheeseburger, silently vowing never to marry. The way she saw it, the man got to boss the wife around. She didn't want some man telling her what to do. She didn't want to be like Mommy, trying to assert herself but having to continually back down. Yet, even though she could see that her parents' relationship was less than ideal, she respected her father. She respected his power. She wanted that power for herself one day. She wanted to grow up to be like him. She wanted to be in control.

"We're going to be the talk of the town," Daddy was going on now, the hardness in his eyes softened as he sold his dream to Mommy, who would have to buy it and be happy for it whether she liked it or not. "I've thought of everything. We'll be secluded, at least for a little while, and we'll have the largest lot in the subdivision. And the view. You're going to love the view, Caro."

"Where is it, Isom?" Mommy asked meekly. "I hope you haven't bought on the river. You know I'm terrified of the river, of something happening to one of the babies."

"See? I knew you'd love it. We'll be overlooking the river. Hell, we'll be overlooking all of Scottsboro. We're building up on July Mountain."

Deb swallowed as fear niggled at the corner of her mind. Two years is a lifetime for a child, and Deb couldn't quite remember what was so scary about July Mountain except that it was something Fat Sarah had said, had warned her about. She could recall sitting in the niche of the oak tree and pretending that the mountain could see her, could watch her. But none of that was real. Fat Sarah had just told her stories about the mountain to keep her penned in the yard, to keep her away from the dangerous roads. She had outgrown Fat Sarah's scary stories and threats. There were enough real problems in her world to worry over without believing a mountain was out to get her. That was ridiculous. Still, moving onto it was not exactly her idea of a dream home.

"I don't want to live on a mountain," she said before she could stop herself.

"Sure, you do, Little Deb," Daddy said. "You're going to love it there. Just you wait and see."

9

The new house was a cedar saltbox with a full basement, stained chocolaty brown tip to stern. It was situated at the top of the mountain, in a crossroads not unlike the position of the green house she could barely remember living in even though they drove right by where it stood on their way home each day. Mommy had been relieved that Daddy had not chosen a bluff lot. She would have worried constantly about Brent tumbling down the mountainside to his death.

Mommy was always worried about ways Brent or Deb could kill themselves. She was always worried about what could go wrong. She was always worried about accidents, particularly ones that would end in drowning. She did not like water. She did not take baths, only showers. She did not go boating, and she had an acute fear of flash floods. Women have an innate sense of their doom. Mommy was attuned to it, yet it still caught her by surprise. At thirty-eight, she would be brought down by a congenital heart condition, drowning in her own blood. It wasn't the water she need fear at all.

This recognition is generational. It is subtle but as solid as a heartbeat, or in Mommy's case, as steady as a ticking clock, counting down the years, days, and hours until destiny is met at last. She knew. We all know. It is a cellular knowledge. Deb was not yet old enough to recognize the call, but she, one day would suffer from the neurosis that develops from a chronic premonition of death. What agony to know the method but not the hour. What exquisite agony to know the hour, but not the method, to feel the bony finger of Death upon the soul, an omnipresent handfast grip. There are periods of relative freedom when the hold does not strangle but, cage-like, defines. Freedom has definitive parameters; freedom is an oxymoron. So goes life, and so goes death.

***

Deb woke in the night. It would be years before she had a true awareness of time or of her appointed hour, and yet she felt unease and a vague sense of loss, even if she did not yet have the ability to articulate it. The time was 2:27 a.m. Deb had a tiny alarm clock in her new bedroom, plush with pink shag carpet. The cotton candy pink curtains were fringed in airy pink pom poms and screened Deb from any prying eyes. She tried not to look at the window in the night, but her eyes were drawn to it, searching, hoping, and fearing the time when she would see something peering back from the deck outside her window.

Her bed was painted pink as well. The walls were pink. Deb was awash in pink, tone-on-tone pink, a little girl's dream room that would become the source of nightmares for years to come. The bed, bathed in a peony-sprigged comforter with a pink Chantilly dust ruffle, anchored the room. Decorator shams rose like rubicund swells on a pink sea. A large collection of unloved dolls hung on the walls like a macabre museum of babies, staring blankly into nothingness, lost in the cotton candy sweetness of the room.

Mommy painted the furnishings, sewed the curtains, and hung the dolls. Deb had received some sort of baby doll for every Christmas and birthday in her memory. Her grandmother was determined that a little girl needed a doll. Mommy was determined that every gift from a grandparent was an heirloom, whether it came from Paris or the local dime store. The dolls hung side by side, in rows along the walls of the bedroom. They populated it with fixed eyes, moving eyes, and cries of "Mama" on the rare occasions they were removed from the wall and rearranged. Deb never played with them. In fact, she despised them, much preferring the growing stuffed animal collection that flanked her on her bed, a kind of force field against the ever-watching eyes of the hateful dolls.

Those wakeful moments in the middle of the night were the worst. The moonlight would play on the wall, animating the dolls. Curls would move in the current of the central air, winking in the bluish half-light from the fluorescent security lamp that protected the garage. Deb would lie stock-still in the middle of the bed, animals on either side of her, and try to blend in. Maybe if the dolls did not recognize the girl beneath the covers, they would not speak to her.

Deb cowered, trying not to make eye contact with the dolls, trying not to look at the window, trying not to look. She made herself invisible as best she could before sleep, once again, captured her. The doll conversations lived somewhere in that land between waking and dreaming. That was a comfort. She could tell herself it was only her imagination. What child doesn't fantasize that her dollies come to life? Nevertheless, she was glad that they were suspended on her wall by nails. They could not wriggle free. They would never have a place with her on the sanctuary of her bed, what little sanctuary that was. Often, after this spout of fear-tinged wakefulness, Deb would fall back into a fitful sleep, and she would dream dreams that did not belong to her. These dreams made her uneasiness around the suspended dolls seem like child's play. So Deb tried to stave off the dreams by recalling stories. Sometimes the stories were innocuous fairy tales, but more often they were remembrances.

"Stay in the bed," Mommy said. "You never know what's creeping around in the night." Caro Ballard found an almost perverse pleasure in "curing" Deb of night walking or wandering. When they had lived in the little, green house in the valley, Deb would occasionally sneak out the back door and bed down in the hollow of what Mommy referred to as the God-forsaken tree. Mommy didn't understand what it was about that tree that drew Deb to it, even against the typical childlike monsters of the night. On the one hand, she was glad Little Debbie exhibited no silly fears of the dark, but on the other hand, fearlessness could breed trouble. She decided Debbie needed a good healthy dose of fear, so she told her stories. She planted the seeds knowing fully Debbie's little imagination would take over and do the rest of the job for her. She certainly didn't want Deb to go wandering alone on the damned mountain, so Mommy cultivated a prickly hedge of fear, a line of defense that would protect them both from something she couldn't define.

"When I was a girl, I used to walk around in the night because it was quiet, and my brothers wouldn't bother me. Nobody could boss me around because the whole world was sleeping. That's when I learned that the whole world doesn't sleep, Deb. There are others who walk in the night, too."

"Who, Mommy?" Deb said, anticipating the possibility of a friend. The move to the top of July Mountain was a lonely one. They were the only family who had bought and built in the subdivision that Daddy had promised soon would have its own store and school for the children.

"No, not friends, Deb." Caro paused for effect and dropped her voice. "Others. Monsters are very much real."

Deb's eyes widened. She was, after all, a fourth grader now, and getting a bit big for such nonsense, but Mommy said it with such conviction, such sincerity, that it gave her pause. The seed was planted.

Caro continued. "That's why I want you to stay tucked tight in your bed at night. They look in the windows at night, searching. They hide under beds, waiting. I wouldn't even hang my arm off the bed if I were you. I don't. What if one of them grabbed you? What if one of them dragged you under the bed?"

Mommy had her attention now.

"I once saw one when I was a girl," she said, "not much older than you are right now. He was a large, sweaty black man. He carried a machete. You know what a machete is, right?"

Deb turned her head slowly. Mommy almost had her cured of night walking.

"A machete is a giant knife, like soldiers use to cut through the jungles or to cut through the enemy. It's about this big." She spread her arms to show the size of the knife. "It could cut your head clean off in a single swipe." Mommy drew her hand across her throat. "Anyway, he was under my bed, waiting. One night, I finally got up the courage to look. I very slowly crept over the edge of the bed and lifted the covers. He was staring back at me, his machete glinting in the moonlight. His eyes were glowing."

"What did you do, Mommy?"

"I put the covers back down and left him there. I knew that if I got off that bed he would have me. His eyes looked hungry. There are rules for night watchers, you know."

"What rules?"

"Well, for one, the bed watchers have to stay under the bed. They have no power beyond the shadow of the bed. If a child steps down or hangs her hand or foot off the edge, they can grab them, drag them under, and eat them. That's where most of the disappearing children go. They don't understand the rules."

"How do you know the rules?" Deb's eyes narrowed. Mommy almost had her, but Deb was sharp, sensing a hole in the explanation.

"He told me. He whispered the rules up through the bed in the darkest part of the night. He told me that he hungered for my bones and my flesh more than anything else he had known. He told me that he had been assigned to me and to those who come after me. The monster under the bed is real, Deb."

"Then why didn't he get me before, when I was little and used to walk out to the tree?"

"Because you were too little to know fear. It's only when you get old enough to recognize fear that a monster waits. His power lies in your fear."

"Then, I just won't be afraid," Deb said, one hand on her hip.

"That's what I thought when I was your age, too," Mommy said and turned back to the TV.

Deb stole a last glance at the hanging dolls, shifted her weight imperceptibly, and drifted away on the thought, *Hell of a bedtime story, Mommy.*

10

The early years on July Mountain seemed idyllic aside from the waking nights. But those seemed fewer as Deb sped toward adolescence. Logic was slowly conquering imagination, and it became easier to deny or even ignore the mountain voices. It became easier to chalk its rumblings to coincidence or to find a feasible explanation that steered her away from the ever-present feeling that something was coming. She learned to cope, to ignore, to rationalize. In that, she was like her mother, but she did not have the luxury of avoidance. Her mother could stay away from water, could escape her fear, but Deb was immersed in hers, and in that immersion, she was able to roam.

The mountain may have eyes, but proximity lends invisibility, just like in her sixth grade class, where she sat on the front row. Mrs. Steadman always looked right over her head, monitoring the rest of the classroom. She could open her novel in her lap and read the day away without even a mild reprimand. She kept quiet, turned in her worksheets, and did as she pleased. She could be overlooked.

The school bus climbed the treacherous mountain road each day to transport her and Brent to and from school. They were the first and last stop, riding just over an hour each morning and afternoon. Daddy had finally cajoled or badgered the county enough to begin an improvement project on the road. At places, it had disintegrated to gravel, and in certain spots, there were more potholes than pavement. The road up the mountain had hairpin turns and steep inclines. There was no shoulder. The woods encroached on the roadbed, threatening to snuff it out of existence if given enough time and neglect by enterprising men.

The road up the mountain was dangerous enough to pose an exciting challenge to the area teenage boys, rednecks, and general adventure-seekers. Only the topmost drop-off sported a guardrail, and it was possible for vehicles to slide off the side of the mountain, tumbling through trees and scrub if they got too reckless. It was necessary to shift into the lowest gear to make the climb. Many cars would not make it to the top of the mountain without at least a little smoke coming off the engine. In all, the mountain climb twisted and turned its way for a little over a mile before making a final ascent to the top. Drivers had to be alert, for many cars careened rather than drove down the mountain, taking the insides of curves like racecar drivers. A slow ascent meant a speedy descent, especially if a driver didn't want to smell burning brake pads.

Near the top of the mountain, the road curved, hugging a steep embankment on one side and a sheer drop on the other. This was where the rusted guardrail offered cursory protection from doom. In the drive off the mountain, an impossibly steep downhill ended in flight if one couldn't make the hard right that followed along the pass. The guardrail ended prematurely in a tangled mass of metal dangling off the cliff, a visible cautionary tale.

The school bus had to gear down one last time before climbing that final hill above the lookout, and the sound carried to the Ballard home, giving Deb enough time to walk the driveway from the front stoop on cold, wet mornings without having to stand out in the elements. The roads on top of the mountain had exotic, rich-sounding names, particularly for Deb: Buena Vista Drive, Monte Vista Drive, July Mountain Boulevard. This would be the place for the elite of Scottsboro to live, their mansions hugging the edge of the mountain with entire walls of windows to showcase the view of the Tennessee

River and the town that appeared picturesque from above. But, for now, those fancy roads were chert and in bad need of grading. The road that the house fronted was deeply veined from the runoff. That was the road that rose to the apex of the mountain with a hill so steep Deb could bear-crawl up it.

The mountain subdivision was laid out not so much in a grid system but with doglegs that traced the ridgelines. Each dogleg converged into July Mountain Boulevard, which really wasn't a boulevard at all, just a plain street. Deb Ballard's childhood home was situated in the hub of the activity. A dogleg shot off along the face of the mountain just before the intersection; except for that, all traffic passed by the house before venturing onward to more dirt roads crisscrossing the mountaintop, as well as a few old logging roads that were impassable without an all-terrain vehicle.

The Ballard home was the first to be built in the subdivision. It was hardly an estate home but was impressive by the standards of the day. It was a thoroughly modern saltbox split-level in chocolate-stained siding with a large, wooden sundeck wrapping around three sides of the house. It was a definite step up from the tiny, green rental house at the foot of the mountain or the apartment complex they had lived in before. Over time, the home would undergo additions, renovations, and transformations that would turn it into a sprawling behemoth. But for the first three years of living on the mountain, it stood as the lone sentinel.

The development stalled. Deb and Brent had the mountain all to themselves. Deb loved to walk through the woods, always watchful for snakes, sometimes venturing over a mile from home. The mountain belonged to her, and she belonged to the mountain. It was a time unlike any other. It was a time of innocence, and Deb was lulled into that false sense of security that familiarity breeds. The mountain had become her home, the threats of the past forgotten in the wonder of the present.

59

11

The double doors that marked the entrance of the house were substantial and unwelcoming. As the saltbox had settled on its foundation, the doors had loosened in their housing enough that a strong wind would rattle them. Sometimes they would swing open unbidden. Deb and Brent were latchkey kids, often home alone for two or three hours before Daddy would pull in the driveway. They were strictly forbidden to answer the door for strangers. The position of the upstairs slider off the dining room allowed them to see anyone who approached the door if they parked in the driveway, which visitors, delivery men, or the poor Jehovah's Witnesses who walked their bicycles up the mountain would naturally do.

They were never home alone after dark, but the afternoons could get lonely, especially since the children were directed to stay inside the home, behind locked doors, until their father arrived. At that time, they would rush outdoors for whatever sunlight was left before dinnertime.

Most afternoons, Brent watched TV or played video games to while away the time, leaving Deb to her own devices. She read or tinkered on the piano. Some days she played the stereo. The stereo was a large wooden cabinet that housed a turntable and an eight-track tape player. It sat in the basement lounge, an area with a fully stocked western-style bar and a pool table that was ideal for parties her parents never had.

She was down in the basement bar, listening to Daddy's Frankie Valli and the Four Seasons eight track when a shadow crossed over the wall. She instinctively turned back toward the sliding glass door. At the same time, she could hear the sounds of space battle in the next room. Someone had walked past the slider. Someone was in the yard.

She ran up the stairs to peek outside of the upstairs slider into the driveway. She had not heard anyone pull up, but if somebody were at the house, they would have driven. The mountain road was too steep and long for anyone with a lick of sense to walk.

There was no car in the driveway. The front door creaked. Deb knew without even looking that the knob was being tried. She was upstairs. Brent was downstairs. And someone was trying to enter the house between them. She dropped out of sight under the dining table as the front door swung open.

Deb heard no sound but the faint blasts of lasers and the beating of her heart loud in her ears. The second step creaked whenever it was stepped on. Mommy had badgered Daddy to repair it, but he said it was just as good as an alarm. Deb listened. She waited. The house had no back stairwell, so there was no way to get to Brent. Whoever was on the landing was making a choice: up or down.

Up the stairs would lead whoever it was to Deb; down the stairs would lead to the unsuspecting Brent. The telephone was across the room in the kitchen area, but Deb was frozen in place. The second step creaked. Deb curled herself between the twin pedestals of the table, ears attuned to the footsteps.

"Go away. Go away!" she shouted inside her mind, too afraid to cry out. She stared at the doorway, waiting to see a shadow cast itself onto the goldenrod carpet. It was shag, like the carpet in her room, and muffled steps if someone were careful, trying not to be heard. She waited some more, but no shadow fell. No one entered, but she could feel someone there. Someone was watching, someone who knew exactly where she was hidden away.

61

"Hey, stupid! You left the door open." Brent came bounding up the stairs, taking them two at a time and making enough noise to raise the dead. He didn't bother himself with closing it. He wasn't the one who opened it in the first place. Just as he was swinging around the banister—Mommy had expressly forbidden that little move—Deb felt it.

A puff of air caught her right in the face. No, it wasn't a puff. It was a breath. Something had breathed on her, crouched in her worthless hiding place below the dining room table. The heavy curtain on the sliding glass door fluttered, a series of ripples down its length, and it was gone as quickly as Brent breezed into the dining room.

"Hey! Where are you? I want a snack before Daddy gets home." As poor as her hiding spot was, Brent didn't see her, at least not immediately. He did see movement behind the curtain, though, bounding immediately into attack position.

"I've got you!" he yelled. Everything with Brent was some sort of yell. Deb's brother did everything with great animation as if he were actually a character in one of the video games he played to the point of obsession. He dove behind the curtain, throwing fabric carelessly to the side and rattling the rings on the rod as he moved down the length of the curtain.

It could have only been a couple of seconds, but time had taken on that frozen quality as Deb remained under the kitchen table, her body practically molded to the pedestal. She was too frightened to cry out, to warn her brother. He was too headstrong to listen. The breath of the thing had taken her voice. She was paralyzed by the smell of it. She could have explained a draft, an eddy, or a sudden breeze. After all, the front door was standing wide open, but it wasn't the air movement that had her in thrall. It was the odor.

The odor was unique, unlike anything she thought she had smelled before. It was a mixture of something like dirt, pinesap, and old bucket water. There was a fetid quality about it that she couldn't quite place. Her grandfather's image popped into her

62

mind. More accurately, it was her memory of his image, for she hadn't thought of him in years, and Mommy rarely spoke of him. She had only visited his gravesite one time, when his sister, Great Aunt Ida, had died and been buried at his feet. Nonny had snickered at that because Papa didn't like his sister all that much in life, and she thought he'd be pleased she'd have to sniff his feet for the hereafter.

All these thoughts and images flashed through Deb's mind as Brent careened through the curtain. Some synapse of memory triggered. It was not really memory, but base instinct, and she recognized the smell. She knew she had smelled it just before her grandfather's accident. It was no accident, she recalled, even though that's how Daddy referred to the incident. She found her voice, springing from her hiding spot.

"Brent! Watch out!"

The curtain rod sprang from its housing, billowing like a sail before bouncing off of something and crashing to the floor.

"Oww!" Brent screamed and began wailing. "Get it off me! Get it off me!" The more he flailed, the more entangled he became in the curtain. Deb pulled handfuls of curtain aside, trying to get to the wriggling mass beneath.

"I can't breathe! I can't breathe!" he hollered, using up air by the gulp. He had always hated to have his head covered. It made him panic. She had used this to her advantage in many a fight with Brent, who was a gargantuan of a nine year old while she was a shrimp of a girl. They made a fairly even match. Deb finally got ahold of an arm and yanked him free of the shroud. Fabric ripped beneath him, caught on something.

"You're gonna be in trouble," he sniffled, a goose egg already rising on his forehead. Deb hugged him tight before he pushed her away. "Knock it off! I'm gonna tell."

"No, you're not, or I'll clobber you. You're gonna help me get this curtain back up before Daddy gets home, or we're both gonna get it." Deb resumed her bossy big sister role and glanced around nervously. The quality of the air had changed. Whatever had been in the room with them was gone.

"Did you fart?" Brent asked after he'd sucked up his snot the way he always did after having a crying fit.

"Yeah. What you gonna do about it?" Deb lied. Brent smelled it, too. It was real. "C'mon. Let's put this curtain back up."

The children worked as a team for once, climbing up on the dining room chairs to get enough height to place the rod back in the cradles hung above the slider. The only evidence of the mishap was a rip in the lining down toward the end. Deb hoped that Mommy wouldn't notice that, and there was a good chance she wouldn't, at least not for a long time. First, it was on the backside of the curtain; second, the way the curtain hung, the rip would be difficult to see from the driveway below. She figured they were pretty safe with the exception of the goose egg.

They put the chairs back in place, and Deb got a piece of ice from the freezer, wrapping it in the soured dishcloth hanging over the sink. "Here. It's a bit stinky, but the ice should take care of your bump. I'm only helping you so we both don't get into trouble. If you say a word about ripping the curtain, I'll give you a lot more than that goose egg," she threatened.

"I'd like to see you try it, butthead," he replied sullenly.

"I'm not the one who cried over getting tangled up in a curtain, sissy. So, hush."

"Well, you shouldn't have been hiding." Brent would never be satisfied unless he had the last word. Deb walked back over to the fridge and pulled a hot dog from the drawer. "Here, eat your hot dog. Daddy will be home soon." She handed Brent his favorite snack: raw hot dogs. Well, they weren't really raw because they had been cooked before at the factory, or so she assumed. He liked them plain, no bun, no ketchup, and cold right out of the fridge. He'd eaten enough of them in the past to rule out any threat of ptomaine poisoning, so she figured one more would be just fine.

"Thanks, idiot," he said, and things were back to normal.

Deb walked out of the kitchen to head toward the bathroom. She needed a little private time to clear her head, and a trip to the john would make that fart all the more plausible. At the foot of the stairs, the front door was closed. The deadbolt was engaged, gleaming through the crack between the doors. Her bowels grumbled, loosening, and she ran to the bathroom, trying to make it to the toilet in time.

12

Samson came to them in the dog days of summer when the Alabama heat can be seen in waves undulating over the fields. He almost didn't make it. Both Deb and Brent got to ride in the truck to pick up Samson, who was kept in a small concrete kennel out behind the house of one of Mommy's distant cousins. Deb vaguely remembered GodLutherYouStink, mostly because his name was so catchy. Brent had no memory of the Saint Bernard at all. The drive to Morgan City was long and hot, especially for excited children who were about to get their very own dog. It didn't help that the air conditioner on the truck sputtered in fits and starts, not doing much better than a balmy ninety degrees in the cab.

"I guess we'll have to ride like a bunch of rednecks," Daddy said, rolling down his window. "Roll your window down, Deb. It'll still be hot, but at least the air will be moving."

Deb rolled her window down and tried not to touch Brent who was sitting in the middle, his bare legs sticky with sweat. He gave her an elbow just for the heck of it.

"Stop it, moron."

"Make me."

"I'll turn this truck around, and that dog can just go to hell," Daddy warned. He blew his horn as he wheeled around the car in front of him. "Get off the damn road, you ugly old bag!" Daddy called to the grandma he was passing. She was squinched up tight to the steering wheel, working hard to keep her car between the guardrails. On either side of the two-lane highway, the backwaters of the Tennessee River lapped. Deb watched as the water flew past, dotted with bass fishermen.

For people touring or driving the route between Scottsboro and Guntersville for the first time, it was a picturesque drive. Highway 79 traced its way along the backwaters banked by Grant Mountain on one side and Sand Mountain looming well across the bottoms. The road was segmented by a series of causeways, most with a backwater view, but a few opening to the river beyond, where barges carried their cargoes toward either Chattanooga or Huntsville. Deb didn't really have a good feel for the geography of the region, but it seemed like the waters crept into every low-lying nook or cranny they could.

New, fancy lake houses and decrepit fishing shacks stood shoulder to shoulder, jostling for the best river views. Boathouses and fishing piers fingered their way out into the water, side by side.

"Why do they put the piers right next to each other, Daddy?" Deb asked as they sped across a gracefully curved causeway. She was looking at the cove side, its waters green with milfoil.

"People want what's theirs. Grownups don't like to share any more than you and Brent do."

"It'd be prettier if it weren't so crowded. People just mess up nature. I can imagine being an Indian, exploring that cove for the first time in my canoe."

"Choctaw, Chickasaw, Cherokee, Creek!" Brent chanted, calling up the Alabama history lessons that his fourth grade teacher had drummed into his head.

"Well, you'd have a mighty hard time paddling that canoe, Little Debbie," Daddy replied. Daddy only called her Little Debbie when he was about to teach her a lesson or whip her. She figured this time it was the former. "You think this water's always been here, squeezing up to the mountains like that? No, ma'am. This here was farmland. Good, rich farmland."

Deb looked dubiously at her father. "Huh? Was there a flood?"

"Now how many floods you ever hear of that don't dry up? Haven't you heard about the Guntersville Dam and the TVA?" Daddy looked over at Brent. "They're teaching you all about the damn good-for-nothing Indians making pottery up in Russell Cave but aren't saying a damn word about how the TVA stole thousands of acres of land all across Jackson and Marshall Counties? Hell, son. The Creeks weren't even from around here. They lived over three hundred miles south of us. Now, they were probably canoeing their way all over the deltas, hunting gators and moccasins, but I can tell you both that there weren't any Indians paddling along what you're looking at right now."

"Well, wasn't the river there?" Brent asked.

"Of course, the river was there. What are you, stupid? I'm talking about the backwaters and the lake." Daddy was never one to spare feelings when it came time to set someone straight, even his own children.

"I like the Indians," Brent said.

"I reckon you might, since you got some Cherokee blood running through you from your mama's side. But you'd best remember an Indian ain't but one step up from a nigger, so I wouldn't be bragging about it if I were you."

"Daddy," Deb interrupted before he got off on a tangent about nigger-lovers. She'd been taught about prejudice at the junior high school. It was like the textbook used her daddy as a model. Of course, she'd never dare say as much. He'd probably slap the taste right out of her mouth. "Tell us about the TVA."

Daddy was happy to oblige as they sped along the highway, passing logging trucks on the double yellows just to get around them. His tale was peppered with epithets and foul language, but Deb was as used to that as she was used to his double standards for boys and girls. It was grownup talk, and he could talk like that if he wanted to, but woe be unto her if she ever

68

used those words herself. That just wouldn't be lady-like, and there was nothing worse than a trashy girl. It was ponderous to keep up with all the rules for righteous living with her daddy barreling headlong into the face of most of them, but she managed.

"Well, let's see. It was the Great Depression and folks in North Alabama, well in most places for that matter, were suffering. There weren't no jobs to be had and people were living mostly off of what they grew in their gardens and just plain meanness. Cotton prices hit bottom and folks just left it to rot in the fields. That's what happened to your granddaddy Levin."

"Was he Mommy's daddy?" Brent asked. He had no memory whatsoever of his grandfather on Mommy's side.

"Yes, doofus. He died when you were a baby," Deb piped in.

"That he did. Right in our back yard, the poor bastard. Right before the cotton prices plunged, they soared, and your granddaddy was gonna get filthy rich. He was so sure of it that he could taste it. And probably did. Your granddaddy was mighty fond of whiskey, you know."

Deb didn't know that. "I just thought he liked to drink cough syrup."

Daddy laughed. "The things a child can remember! That was only after your grandmama poured out all his whiskey. He'd fake a cough and drink cough syrup by the bottle so he could get liquored up to spite her. But that was years after my story."

"Anyway, your granddaddy had his cotton all loaded up, setting on his flatbed with his whole field-full of bales waiting in the barn. Cotton prices had been rising steadily for two weeks while he about broke his back getting it all in. It was near about the end of October 1929, and he figured he'd house it until the first of November and make himself a bundle.

69

"The stock market crashed, and your granddaddy lost his shirt and his land to boot. The story goes that he near about stroked out and, in his rage, set fire to the barn with the flatbed setting right in it. What he didn't know was that your Uncle Bedford was curled up sound asleep in the cab of that truck. He wasn't but a little fellow, about five or six years old. He was excited about going to the cotton gin and seeing all that cotton turned into money, like his daddy had promised. Well, he went to Heaven instead. It about killed your grandparents. I didn't know them until I was grown, but folks say it changed them forever."

"That's really sad," Deb responded.

"Did it burn him up?" Brent asked, eager for the gory details.

"Nah, it just cooked him like he was in an oven. That's why you should never sleep down in the floorboard of a vehicle. You never know what could happen," Daddy replied.

"Anyway, your mom was just a baby when this happened, and the family moved in with your grandmama's folks, which was a mighty big dish of crow for a man to eat. Broke him, they did. And then had the gall to publicly forgive him up in front of the church for killing their grandson. It's their folks we're going to get the bulldog from."

Daddy was on a roll now. The speedometer on the truck was creeping higher and higher while Daddy told his story. The deeper in he got, the faster he drove, pausing only to cuss the damned loggers who were tearing up the road with their overloaded trucks and who should be fined or jailed or shot, according to his mood as he passed them on the narrow road.

"That's how the sons of bitches at the TVA got ahold of your granddaddy. He needed something to regain his manhood and had enough experience tinkering with wiring to get hired on as an electrician. They hired men out of most every family in the Tennessee Valley, with promises of a steady paycheck that would put food on the table, and in your granddaddy's case, get his family the hell out of his in-laws' house."

"The Guntersville Dam project provided much-needed jobs, but the price was high. The TVA talked about nothing but giving folks a chance, giving folks a future, giving folks a way. All the while, they were taking with the other hand. They bought out the farmers at bargain-basement prices, paying a fraction of what the land should have been worth. Those who wouldn't sell were forced out. Your granddaddy helped clear the land, as those TVA bastards put it.

"Deep down, at the bottom of the water all over this area, are farmhouses, buried by the flood of progress. The TVA made a big show of relocating folks, providing housing for them, and respecting their dead, buried in family plots on family land the way they did back then. But your granddaddy always swore they didn't move nothing but the headstones. He told darker tales, too. By the time it was said and done, the river had swollen its banks and created the lakes, coves, and backwaters like you see now, Lake Guntersville being the biggest of all. He had long since lost his land before the TVA stepped in, but he still thought of it as his. We're coming up on Claysville right now. That's where your granddaddy farmed his cotton, somewhere at the bottom of the lake. That's where he buried your uncle, and to have heard your granddaddy tell it, that's where he still is today."

The truck came to a brief stop before Daddy made the turn onto US 231 into Guntersville. Lake Guntersville opened up beside them as Deb imagined fields of cotton where the water flowed today.

"Hey, look! The bridge!" shouted Brent. A rise in the road showed the top of the metal bridge that spanned the Tennessee River, or the part of it that spilled over into Lake Guntersville. Like a mountain pass, the bridge connected Claysville to Guntersville, both towns sitting on their respective hilltops.

"Hold your breath! Hold your breath!" Brent took a big gulp of air before the truck left the safety of the land for the enormous bridge. The bridge was built on huge pilings that dove hundreds of feet deep to the river bottom. Steel beams rose in a maze above the highway to support the weight of cars and trucks traversing it. The bridge was frighteningly narrow. Two eighteen-wheelers only had a couple of feet of clearance on either side as they passed one another. Daddy said he'd heard of side mirrors being knocked off as trucks met.

Although the road was just as wide as it was on the ground, the height and the cage-like construction of the bridge created an optical illusion. Many drivers were so claustrophobic that they would split the center line if no other car was meeting them, gripping their steering wheels with both hands to steady their nerves and their vehicle.

It seemed miraculous that no more people died than actually did on that bridge known for its near misses. Maybe it was the extra caution drivers took, going more slowly. Maybe the fear of having to choose between the agonies of a head-on collision or a death-plunge into the swirling waters of the Tennessee River kept people alert.

"Don't put your arm out the window, Deb. It may get knocked off!" Daddy warned cheerfully as he accelerated through the bottom and into the incline of the bridge.

Brent's cheeks were puffed out like a trombone player's. A car up ahead straddled the center line. Daddy was bearing down hard on it and laid on his horn. "Get over, asshole!" he hollered, flashing his lights. They were approaching the crest of the bridge, like a giant parabola. If the truck were up to speed, they'd get the brief sensation of floating as they raced over the top of the hump. Deb raised her feet off the floorboard so she'd float.

The asshole ahead inched over toward the spanners and Daddy swerved into the passing lane just as they reached the

72

apex of the bridge. "Woo hoo!" Daddy yelled. "Oh, shit!" A logging truck was chugging up the incline, directly in their path.

"Hang on, kids!"

Brent ducked into Deb's lap forgetting all about holding his breath. Deb's feet rose instinctively as if she could kick away the truck they were barreling toward. Daddy swerved back into his lane with inches to spare, but overdid it just a bit. The side mirror slapped a girder, shot straight into the air, and arced off into the river below.

Daddy had finally put both hands on the wheel but was laughing. "That was a close one, huh? Best not tell your mom how I knocked the mirror off. Sure am glad you listened, Deb. That could've been your arm feeding the catfish right now," Daddy chuckled, checking his rearview mirror as the logger topped the bridge and drove on. "Let's go get your dog."

Twenty minutes later, they'd climbed Brindlee Mountain and were on the outskirts of Union Grove when Daddy took a turn down a road with a sign that said Guntersville Dam. They dropped off the backside of the mountain and approached the dam. Fishermen dotted the banks, fishing for crappie. Even a few black folks were casting their lines.

"They'd best be over this mountain before dark," Daddy said while smiling and nodding at an ancient man with hair like a cotton ball and teeth so white they made his skin look like midnight. Boulders, riprap really, lined the bank to corral the river when the TVA opened the spillways. Daddy parked the truck, throwing the lever into P and exiting in one smooth motion. Deb and Brent followed Daddy on foot as he picked his way between rocks down to the water's edge.

"The best fishing is right up against the dam, but you sure wouldn't want to swim there. They say there are catfish trolling the bottoms large enough to swallow a man. I've seen pictures of fishermen who've snagged a cat in excess of two hundred pounds."

The mighty Tennessee churned against the mountain of concrete looming over them.

"Daddy, what if the dam broke right now?" Brent asked, eyes upturned.

"Well, Brent, if your mom has the right of it, we'd be having lunch with Jesus today instead of at the Burger Chef. But don't worry. It's not going to break. Let me show you something," Daddy replied.

Brent forgot all about the danger of the dam breaking as Daddy indicated an approaching barge. "What do you think that barge is going to do, son?"

"It looks like it's going to try to come over the dam!" Brent jumped up and down in excitement.

"Well, you're right, but it's not going to just fall over the spillway. It's going to go through a lock." Daddy enjoyed being the bastion of knowledge on this trip to get a distantly related dog. He kept up a running commentary for both of us, likening the lock to a giant bathtub. Even Brent had enough sense to know Daddy was joshing when he talked about the barge captain sending the cabin boy down to the bottom to pull a giant plug.

They watched the barge slowly make its way through the lock and resume its journey toward Huntsville or beyond. Deb wanted to watch a barge climb the dam to go the other direction, but there was not enough time, and they were expected in Morgan City to get the dog before the morning was out.

They got back in the sweltering truck, each with a Coke from the bait store by the dam. Daddy dropped some peanuts down in his Coke to fizz and flavor the soft drink. "Want some nuts?" he asked as he pulled out of the parking area. Deb took a handful, enjoying the salty taste of peanuts with her drink but not in it. The carbonation ate the nuts. There was something just plain unpleasant about that.

They drove along through Dead Man's Curve without mishap or seeing any dead men, and Daddy told the story of how it got its name.

"When the engineers designed this curve, they banked it the wrong way. That's what makes it an especially dangerous curve. I've never heard of a dead man here, but these fools that built their house in the heart of the curve had their kid get run over. Serves them right for picking a stupid place to build a house." Daddy had little sympathy for anyone.

Although Deb knew he held deep prejudices, she recognized he was an equal-opportunity bigot. He pretty much detested anyone who wasn't just like him, believed the same things he believed, or opposed him in any way. That's why he and Mommy didn't get along and hadn't gotten along in her memory. That was probably why they kept opposite work schedules, but Deb didn't know that for sure. She loved both of her parents, faults and all.

Deb didn't really know why Mommy hadn't come along on this trip since it was her family they were going to see to get the dog. She was not working today. Maybe it was just too crowded in the truck, or just too hot.

When they arrived at the house, they didn't even get invited inside or offered a cool drink. Samson was out back in the kennel, barking his head off. He was a boxer bulldog, brown but beginning to gray a bit around the jowls. He had a powerful head and ears that pointed straight to the sky. He was a dog to be reckoned with.

"You kids best stay in the truck," Mommy's cousin Mark ordered as he leashed Samson from within the kennel. Samson growled at him, and Mark cursed him. "That's the last time that dog will growl at me. If it's a guard dog you wanted, Ballard, it's a guard dog you're getting. Samson's a true son of a bitch, and that bitch was the best guard dog I've ever had. You just gotta slap him around a bit so he knows who's boss, and he'll tear anything up that comes near."

75

"That's exactly what I'm looking for. He know any commands?" Daddy asked.

"Don't need none but to be let loose. He knows what to do; I guarantee it. This is one mean son of a bitch." Mark took what appeared to be a one hundred dollar bill from Daddy.

Daddy lifted Samson into the back of the truck and chained him to the toggle mounted on the rim of the cargo bay. He seemed docile until Mark approached him and said, "Good riddance, you sorry son of a bitch."

The hairs on the bulldog's back stood, and he growled deep and low at his former master. When Deb looked into the dog's eyes she could see that Samson knew he'd not only been sold; he'd been saved.

13

Samson nearly died of heat exhaustion before the Ballards could get him home. When they finally pulled into the driveway atop July Mountain, he was panting, eyes glazed. He refused to get up, or couldn't get up, even after Daddy unchained him against Cousin Mark's specific warnings.

"Brent, go get your mother. Deb, get the hose. Be quick about it, both of you," Daddy ordered as he shoved a bowl of water under Samson's nose. The dog snorted but refused to drink.

Deb handed her father the water hose. "Is he going to die?"

"He might. We're going to try to keep that from happening. I spent good money on him. Now run back, and turn on the faucet."

By the time Deb got back to the truck, Daddy was squirting water onto the driveway, waiting for it to cool down. In an Alabama summer, the hose water runs hot for a couple of minutes before cooling to a comfortable temperature. Mommy and Brent were back with a stack of old beach towels by the time Daddy started gently dousing the dog. He didn't want to startle him, but he needed to get the dog cooled down and drinking.

"Here, Isom. Let me soak the towel." She kept a beach towel folded. After it was sopping wet, she placed it under the dog's head. "What's his name?" Mommy asked.

"Samson," said Brent.

"Well, let's hope he's strong just like the Samson from the Bible," replied Mommy. She had begun to rub down his legs with another wet towel.

"Careful. Mark said he's a nipper," Daddy said as she neared the dog's head. Samson thrust out his tongue and gave her hand a single, dry pass. Mommy moved her towel in small circles, massaging and cooling the dog.

"Kids, come over and help. Keep quiet, and don't make any quick moves. Be deliberate," Mommy instructed. She began to sing a lullaby. Daddy picked up at a hum and before long, the whole family was crooning to the dog, rubbing and watering the animal right there in the back of the truck. All four of them worked in harmony for the first time in a very long time. Deb thought, *This is what the families in paintings are like. This is what Norman Rockwell would draw if he were drawing us.* When Samson wagged his stub of a tail, Deb knew he was going to be fine, a fine dog indeed.

***

Samson never so much as snarled at the family, but woe be unto anyone who stepped into the yard. He kept watch, accompanying Deb and her mother on their long walks along the mountain roads. He discouraged deliverymen, mailmen, and the like. The vet had to make visits to their home for his checkups after he almost caused a riot in the veterinarian's office. He tore loose from his leash and had all but eviscerated a cat before the vet popped him with a sedative.

Samson hated motorcycles most of all. Mark had ridden a Honda, and Daddy had voiced suspicions that he must've run at the dog in its kennel. Deb imagined the motorcycle chucking gravel and grass at the trapped dog while her nasty uncle or cousin or whoever he was cussed and laughed. She had never even heard of him before Daddy took them to rescue Samson and didn't figure to hear of him again. No wonder Samson

78

hated motorcycles. He didn't want to go back to that life ever again.

By the time Deb came to love and be loved by Samson, another family had finally moved onto July Mountain. Deb was disappointed that their children had already grown up, and she remained secluded; but truth be told, she liked having the mountain to herself. Samson, on the other hand, had a vendetta to settle. Mrs. Pierce drove a Volkswagen Beetle that sounded a lot like a motorcycle, at least the dog seemed to think so. When she drove off the sharp hill past the house, Samson sprinted out of the yard, hell-bent on biting the tires off the car. He attacked without fail, and Mrs. Pierce told Daddy she thought Samson aimed to kill her, but she was wrong about that. His rage wasn't directed at Mrs. Pierce at all. When she drove her husband's sedan, Samson barely lifted his head. The Beetle, however, never failed to send him into a rampage. He charged the moving vehicle with teeth bared. Sometimes he would get in front of the car, and Mrs. Pierce would blow her horn, stop the car, and sit crying until Daddy came out with a leash and dragged Samson out of her way.

"You ought to just run him down next time," Daddy said, shaking his head. It was difficult to believe that a dog could bully a woman armed with a two-thousand pound vehicle. He'd cuss Samson on those days, threatening to run him down himself, but Deb knew he didn't really mean it.

It became a kind of comedy, Mrs. Pierce laying on her horn from way up the hill. Of course, this only enraged Samson more…Mrs. Pierce driving the long way around the subdivision in hopes of sneaking past before he had a chance to get into his defensive stance. He'd stand his ground right in the middle of the street. She tried to make it look like she was going to run him over, but she would swerve around the dog at the last second or just stop to cry in frustration. Finally, Mrs. Pierce got tired of the trauma of trying to drive her Beetle and traded the car for another with a quieter engine. Samson never so much as barked her way again.

Samson also had a healthy hatred toward cats. He chased one tom across the deck and through the railing without hesitation. The twelve-foot drop didn't even faze him. He just rolled and treed that cat. Many a stray cat met its doom at the jaws of Samson. Squirrels, chipmunks, wildcats, and the occasional snake also fell victim to Samson's unwavering protection of the Ballard family. Deb believed Daddy couldn't have found them a better dog anywhere.

Samson did not always emerge from his adventures unscathed. He wore his battle scars proudly as his muzzle went from salt and pepper to gray. His left ear got chewed almost to the nub, and he developed arthritis. He curled himself into a C whenever Deb approached as if he couldn't decide which part of his body needed petting the most, and she loved him for it.

Samson gave Deb courage, and she trusted him to keep away whatever it was that had peered at her under the table that day Brent tangled himself in the curtains. Samson held up his end of the bargain. Sometimes, deep in the night, she would hear him growl, low and mean. He walked the deck like a captain guarding his ship. It was an excellent vantage point. The height plus the ferocity of his growls would make anyone think twice about approaching the sleeping family.

Deb heard him pad across the deck when she woke in the early morning hours to the moonlight's illumination of the hanging dolls. As she floated in her sea of pink, watching the heads shift and dresses flutter when the air-handling unit kicked in, she felt his presence. His stubby-tailed rump swept the wall three times as he prepared for sleep. She listened to him bed down on the deck, wedging himself tightly against the wall beneath her bedroom window, protecting her from whatever terrors roamed the night. He was a good dog.

14

The mountain never seemed to change. Seasons would come and go, new houses began to dot the overlooks, but the mountaintop subdivision never really gained a foothold. The drive up was too treacherous, and although Deb had never known of anyone running off the road and getting killed, the propensity for disaster seemed to hang in the air as drivers navigated the sharp turns and inclines. No store was built. Neither was a private school for the children of July Mountain, who barely numbered into the teens at the height of the mountain's popularity. Some of the roads eventually were blacktopped, including July Mountain Boulevard, which never reached the grandeur of the tree-lined artistic rendering on the brochure Mommy kept in the top drawer of the repurposed chest of drawers at the head of the stairs. That drawer housed an abundance of brochures of places she'd like to visit one day when they had "made it." A few of them, like a Caribbean cruise, came to fruition, but most of them remained renderings of the imagination similar to the idyllic picture of July Mountain Boulevard. It was a drawer full of if onlys, almosts, and nice tries.

Occasionally, Deb pulled out the drawer to leaf through the brochures and clippings. She loved to organize, make lists, and plans. The only rule from Mommy was that she toss nothing away. So Deb sat contentedly on the landing at the top of the stairs with stacks of papers spread out around her. She had a pile for Places We've Been, Places We'll Go, and Places We

Like. Another series of stacks were for People We Know, Famous People, and Dead People.

The clippings, brochures, playbills, tickets, and programs dated back from when they first moved to July Mountain. As Mommy climbed the stairs after her eleven p.m. nursing shift was over, she would set her purse on the chest of drawers, and drop her evidence of living into the drawer just like she was making a deposit at the bank. She even called it the Proof Drawer.

The Ballard family had "made it" to the point where Mommy no longer nursed on the weekends, and Daddy traveled to those college football games instead of watching them on TV. They continued in their tag team approach to parenting, which both Deb and Brent learned to work to their own advantages. In a way, the children had it made as well.

But it was lonely up on the mountain. The other children who lived nearby were either much older or much younger than Deb…or they were boys. What she longed for was to be able to ride her bicycle to a friend's house, share secrets, and be part of a neighborhood. Brent had that. The July Mountain kids were just the right age for him, and they rode herd over the mountain, raiding the snack cabinets from one house after another. Sometimes, Deb would join the fun, but she had begun to feel silly pretending to be a superhero or replaying space battles from the movies.

The terrain on July Mountain afforded biking in spurts. She pushed her way up some of the bigger hills, and a few were too sharp to ride down comfortably. Nevertheless, Deb would take her bike to roam. It was a sweet freedom, being completely alone with the exception of Samson who trailed at a distance, giving her some space but keeping a watchful eye.

She contemplated taking a ride as she sat with the papers spread around her. She liked to reach up blindly into the drawer and pull out a handful of papers. It added to the mystery and discovery. Her fingers touched plastic, not the slick paper of a brochure, but the flimsy plastic of a sandwich bag. She brought it down out of the drawer.

Inside the plastic was what appeared to be a very old newspaper article, yellowed and brittle with age. Some of the print was faded, but the headline was still readable and caught her attention.

"Clemence Peak Deaths"

Deb went to Brent's room to steal his magnifying glass. He kept it in the bottom drawer of his desk along with a postcard of a woman with her breasts exposed. Mommy and Daddy didn't know about his postcard, but she did. If he became too much of a jerk, it would mysteriously appear where it and he would be found out. Everybody in her house had secrets, and the afternoons at home alone, and whole days in the summer, gave her the opportunity to pry. It was simple with Brent either glued to a video game or off playing space cadet adventures with his buddies. Deb collected the secrets like her mother collected her brochures and snippets of proof. Only Deb wasn't dumb enough to toss them in a drawer. She wasn't sure what Mommy was providing proof of, but Deb did not yet discern that proof can be a protection. For now, she saw her mother's Proof Drawer as mostly a time capsule, random in its contents.

Deb sat back down amongst the piles of paper with the magnifying glass in hand. Parts of the article were faded beyond all hope of reading, and the paper was in danger of crumbling to nothing in her hands, but she could make out a few words. The story wouldn't come together, though. The top of the paper read *Crow Town Chronicle*. She had never heard of a place called Crow Town and wondered why her mother had added this to her collection. It was too old to be some place Mommy wanted to go and too old to commemorate some place Mommy had been.

The date beneath the banner read "July 31, 18—" The last part of the date had been smudged away by time or a careless finger. As best she could tell, something terrible had happened

83

at a bordello, which she decided must be what people used to call boarding houses back before people advanced to apartment complexes and condominiums. A child died. There was a fire. Even with the magnifying glass, the article was proving near impossible to read.

Deb turned the page over at the fold, afraid it might disintegrate if she actually tried to unfold it. The flip side of the clipping was a photograph. A figure stood with a child in hand. Maybe the dead child? Deb peered through the magnifying glass to inspect the faces. Something about the lady's eyes rang familiar.

Deb dropped the glass and sprang backward from the article, scattering her neat stacks of Mommy's Proof. A few fluttered off the balcony to the basement staircase below. It was hard to catch her breath.

The woman in the photograph was the woman from her nightmares, when Deb dreamed those stories that were not her own. The child's face was a mirror of her own.

When Deb dropped the magnifying glass, it gashed the brittle paper. The photograph ripped. The faded face of the child was ruined.

Deb's fingers shook as she put the article back in its sandwich bag. Maybe Mommy wouldn't notice the damage. After all, it was well down in the pile of documents from the drawer, and although she had seen Mommy place items in the drawer, she had never witnessed her taking items out of the drawer for inspection.

Quickly, Deb gathered the whatnot of the drawer and piled it willy-nilly on top of the article. She buried it in the past beneath dream vacations, programs for school productions, stubs from the rock concerts her parents attended, and obituaries for townspeople and distant kin, but the image found its way into that place in her mind where she stored her secrets, even if she didn't understand quite what it was or would become. All she knew was that the image had great significance, a

84

significance that would define her future. It was forever burned into her memory, for as long as a forever could last.

15

Deb was not seeing through her own eyes as she dreamt, but rarely did she. Her dreams were Technicolor cinematographic reels in which she played multiple roles, switching narration and point of view as easily as changing into a different pair of jeans. And she remembered her dreams, at least for a little while—if not vividly, then at least in distinct impressions that left her ecstatic, victorious, or terrified in turn. Deb had heard the story that people who dream that they die also die in real life, but it was an old wives' tale, for she had died many deaths in her dreams. She had lived many lives, but until the July Mountain night terrors came, she had ultimately been in control.

Her dreamscape was one of masterful play. She exercised her imagination, played out her fears, and faced her hopes. In her dreams, she found answers, but she also found questions.

For almost a year, she kept a dream diary, whispered in those late/early hours when she huddled under the multiple stares of her unloved doll collection. It was more of a recording than a diary. She had taken Daddy's business memo tape recorder, the one he replaced because he thought he lost it, and she whispered quietly into it when she woke.

Speaking into the voice recorder soothed her and seemed to lull the ever-watching dolls into their open-eyed slumber. When she spoke, she couldn't hear their quiet voices imploring her, making suggestions that couldn't be labeled anything other than evil.

Mommy discovered the device when changing Deb's linens one Saturday morning. She sat down on the corner of the bed, holding onto the pink bedpost, bare toes digging in the pink shag. She pressed play and Deb's voice, tinny and childlike, filled the room with a remembrance of a dream....

"I am a mommy at the funeral of my child. The sadness is choking me, threatening to pull me down into the grave with my baby. I want to go. I hear people talking around me but can't seem to concentrate on any of it. It is like hearing someone shout when you are underwater. Everything is distorted. Everything moves differently. That's what it's like when your baby dies; you go through the motions, but they don't feel the same. Food does not taste the same. You want the earth to swallow you instead. Sometimes, the earth will give you your wish. Not this time. I am a mommy wrapped in sadness, a sadness that will never be happy again...."

Deb's recorded voice was ragged, as if she'd been weeping, or was about to at any moment. The real-time Deb sat in the rocking chair in the corner of the room, feeling completely and totally violated. Her dreams showed her heart of hearts, and her mother was playing them out loud.

Caro must have sensed her duress. "Deborah, go get your brother's headphones." Mom had no intention of stopping the listening to the recorder, but she had enough pity in her to not play it out loud. Deb was squirming inside her own skin by the time she returned with the headset, a large puffy, black headpiece that made Mommy resemble Princess Leia as she settled on the bed to listen. Mommy pointed back at the chair and Deb sat, too worried to rock.

Mommy's eyes bore holes into her as she listened, her fingers picking at a pill in the pink comforter. She assessed Deb as she listened to the sleepless voice intonate for almost an hour. When, after what seemed like an eternity, the device clicked itself off, Mommy still sat there a full five minutes, unmoving but with her attention fully focused on her daughter.

"Shut the door, Deb, and lock it," Mommy ordered. Deb obeyed. She was much more disquieted by her mother's equanimity than by the screaming fit she anticipated. She detected no frustration or anger in Mommy's voice, only a tired resignation.

"Deb, we share a unique ability, one that neither your daddy nor your brother has," she began. "You notice things other people overlook. You form impressions that, however unlikely, are often exactly right. You see into people. I've known you possess this quality for a very long time and have tried to subdue it because it's a gift that comes with a price I don't want you to have to pay. We can make things happen, you and I...not in a parlor trick kind of way, not like Luke Skywalker learning to use "The Force" while blindfolded, but in a chain reaction, a reaction we orchestrate whether we mean to or not."

Deb had never heard Mommy talk this way before. She had always been aloof, too busy for silliness or heart-to-heart talks. Deb sat stock-still, rapt. She never considered that her vivid dreaming was anything other than an active imagination. Seeing into people, as Mommy called it, was as simple as reading the pages of a book. She just happened to be an excellent reader.

"You must understand that your lifetime will be fraught with pain because you cannot *un*see. You must understand that they will kill you if they root you out, and that they will always be on the hunt. What you can do is the most natural thing in the world; your mind is tuned to the past...I think you are starting to recognize that...and tied to the present. You can change the future, but you can't change *your* future. That is already set; fair and unfair are not even considered in this equation.

"Do you know why I fear water, Deb? It has nothing to do with an inexplicable phobia that makes your daddy think I'm neurotic, does it?" Mommy asked.

"You will die by drowning," Deb replied unblinking.

88

"What about you, Deb? What shall claim you?"

"2:27," Deb responded. "I don't know how, but I know when."

"You find ways to live with it. Some call it a sight. Some call it ESP—that name is pretty safe. If people notice your awareness, you can call it ESP, and you'll only be labeled as a little quirky, not even wacko. We can thank Hollywood for that." Mommy still held to the bedpost as if she intended to root herself there.

"How do you live with it?" Deb asked, relieved that maybe she wasn't the only one who heard things, who saw things that weren't there, who could initiate things if she really wanted to.

"I work. I help other people. I nurse. That keeps me off this mountain most of the time, but it also keeps me away from you. Until I heard this....," Mommy indicated the dream diary, "I thought you had been passed over. I thought after my daddy and the tornado, it had run its course. I was wrong. Why didn't you say anything, Deb? Why didn't you tell me?"

"I don't know. I didn't want to be crazy. I didn't think you'd believe me. I didn't really believe me, anyhow. Most of the time, there's some other explanation." The tears had started coming now.

"You're right. That's how it works. It wedges doubt between you and the truth, between you and what you know. Then it will pick away until you think you are making the decision, but you are really doing as it bids. Of course, you'll be the one left to clean up the mess in the end."

"What are you talking about, Mom?" Just like that, Mommy's name grew up along with Deb.

"The voices whispering inside your head, the dreams. I thought I had you protected, swathed in pink—the color of tender innocence—and surrounded by a legion of watchful eyes." Mom swept her hand across the room to indicate the dolls hanging from nails along the walls.

"I hate those dolls," said Deb.

89

"And that is why they have failed you," Mom replied. "But keep them up. They can still be useful."

"And I hate pink." Deb was drunk on sullenness.

"The pink is a shield against the darkness roaming in the night. It is both a haven and a prison. It locks you in, but it also locks others out."

"Then why do I have such dreams? Why do the dolls speak? Why do I fear what lies beneath my bed?" Deb blurted through her tears, trying to understand. Her mother's voice was perfectly calm, but her vice-like grip on the bedpost gave her away. Her mother was afraid. Was she afraid for her, or was Mom afraid of her?

"You've brought all of those things in here with you, Deb. You've given them strength on this tape. You've made them breathe."

"You're telling me that it's my fault?" Deb was incredulous.

"No. I'm telling you that you must learn to control the voices in your head. You must be certain you know which voices are yours and which are not. You must be vigilant or risk losing yourself. Now, show me," Mom instructed.

"Show you what?"

"Make the dolls talk."

"I can't." Deb's voice became meek, defeated.

"This tape recorder says you can. It's proof. So, show me."

"Why don't you show me?" Deb challenged. This was the longest conversation she could ever remember having with her mother, who had always been distant. If she wanted proof, she was going to have to make herself worthy.

"Ha!" Mom said, "There's that Ballard coming out in you. I'm not one for parlor tricks, but if you insist..."

Mom cast her glance to the mirror above Deb's pink dresser. It was an antique dresser with mercury dotting its edges. Deb looked into the mirror. The mercury traced its way to the center. A figure began to emerge from the darkened glass,

90

much like a Polaroid photo when Deb shook it to bring up the exposure. The figure took the shape of a woman, a woman from the olden days—not just a hundred years ago olden, but many hundreds of years ago.

The woman wore a kirtle belted with fur. Her hair enveloped her like a golden shroud, long and straight, hanging to her thigh. She held a child by the hand, a miniature of herself, with the same flowing hair. Her eyes were hazel, but Deb knew they had that quality of changing from green to gold to blue, according to the light.

As the figure's face came into full focus, Deb gasped. It was the woman from her dreams, from the article she'd found in Mom's Proof Drawer, but something wasn't right. If Deb could find a word to express what she intuitively knew, she would have used "anachronistic" to describe the image formed in her bedroom mirror.

"Her name is Renae Clemence," Mom said flatly. "She is your grandmother ageless."

"But it's the same woman in the news article," Deb was confused.

"So you've discovered it. Yes, Deborah. It is the last recording of her image I have found. When that photograph was taken, she had been dead well over four centuries. Now look in the mirror again."

The mercury retreated to the mirror's edges, and the image of Clemence and the child faded. Deb's own face was coming forth, not really a reflection yet, but a refraction of the dissipating image. Deb pulled on the elastic of her ponytail and let her hair drop, long, stick-straight tresses that lay perfectly flat against her head. The resemblance was as clear as her image had now become. The mirror was just a mirror.

"Your turn," Mom said, ignoring the thousand questions that were swirling in the hazel of Deb's eyes. She sat back down on the bed, clearly expecting Deb to perform.

91

Deb returned to the pink rocking chair and closed her eyes. She reached into her mind and focused her imagination on the dolls. Nothing happened.

"Quit faking, Deborah, and concentrate," Mom ordered. Her voice had a strident ring to it, as if she didn't really want to see this demonstration but felt compelled to watch nevertheless.

Deb took a deep breath and found that place in her mind, or maybe it was her soul, where the impossible fell under her dominion. Talking Tootie, the only doll she had ever loved, began to thrash against the nail holding her to the wall. Mrs. Beasley turned her head. A platoon of Barbies began wriggling, helplessly pinned in place.

"C'mon, Deborah. Let's hear them speak. Command them." Mom grasped the bedpost with both hands now but relentlessly urged Deb forward.

The dolls began quietly. "Little Debbie, Debbie, I love you," said Talking Tootie.

"Mama!" called out another.

"Deb, Deb, I want you," intoned a nameless doll in singsong.

"Let's play hide and seek."

"I see you!"

"You are ugly and stupid. You'll never be good enough."

"Don't look out the window."

"Don't look under the bed."

The comments from the dolls rose to a cacophony, a cafeteria full of school children, their voices loud, snippets of conversation becoming clear as others blended. The dolls called out to Deb. The dolls spoke to one another. The dolls writhed on the wall, struggling to free themselves.

"Enough!" Mom ordered, and the dolls fell immediately silent, immediately inanimate. A single china doll dropped from the wall, its head shattering on the corner of the pink chest of drawers, littering the piled carpet with shards. Deb opened her eyes and looked at her mother, the sudden silence deafening.

92

"That one wasn't your voice," Mom said with disgust as she indicated the broken china doll. "You must heed the voices and search out the ones not your own if you want any chance, girl. Now, show me what you can really do."

Deb could hardly believe that she, she had made the dolls speak. She had brought them to life. Deb could hardly believe that her mother just sat on the corner of the bed, feigning calmness but remaining firmly in control of her emotions, her fear. Deb closed her eyes again, reached deep within, finding that mental switch that brought fancy to life. She rose effortlessly and tapped the ceiling.

"Sit down!" Mom shrieked, shaken. "That's too much. They'll kill you for that. They'll lock you away forever. Holy shit, child! Don't ever show anyone that part of you again. Not even me. That has to be what Clemence wants from you, her blood legacy, and you showing it off like it's the most natural thing in the world.

Mom strode over to the rocking chair, towering above Deb. "I can do things, too, Missy," she hissed. "You'd better believe it. Clemence is coming, and there will be little I can do to stop her. You must protect your family, and the first way you'll do it is by never performing that little feat again." Mom was mere inches from Deb's face, spraying her with spittle in her sudden aggressiveness. She gripped Deb by the chin, painfully.

"Do you understand? People will try to kill you if they find out your secret, our secret. You can't let Clemence grab hold of your mind. She won't kill you, but she'll take you if you let her, and then you might as well be dead. Lock it all away. Lock it tight."

"You're hurting me," Deb squeaked as the tears rolled down her face.

"And I'll hurt you more if you put Brent in danger," Mom spat. "I should've taken care of you when you killed my daddy and then knocked the babysitter's head half off. Oh, I knew then it wasn't the storm that got her, but I held out hope. I hoped you could grow beyond it, but now I see you've been nursing the evil all along, sucking at it like it's a sugar tit, Clemence just biding her time."

Mom's voice instantly became insipid, syrupy with a gentleness that was far more frightening than the threats she had just made. She released her vice-like grip on Deb's chin and smiled.

"You are Deborah from now on, like I named you to begin with, full of the wisdom of the ages. Use it, and maybe we'll all survive what's coming our way. I was hoping you'd be spared, but Clemence is past due for another appearance. I never wanted to have a daughter, but here you are, and the blood has not been washed."

Mom rose and began picking up the shards of china doll. Using a sharp edge, the piece that was once the doll's hand-painted eye, she ripped the cellophane from the cassette diary. "Our secret is a dangerous one, Deborah. It can destroy us both. Maybe it can be our salvation as well. Think on that while you work."

As Mom reached the door, she turned back to Deborah. "It's a chilly day. I think I'll start a fire." She indicated the cassette and the remains of the doll. "You will join me when you're done." Mom passed through the door, her eyes a mixture of pity, fear, and determination. She closed the door behind her with great tenderness, shutting Deborah inside. When her hand released the doorknob, every doll plunged to the carpet. Deborah began the meticulous task of hanging up her own defenses.

Part Two

Mother

16

Her original name was Clemenceau, in grasping fealty to the lord of the manor near where she was born. She was a bastard daughter with an uncanny resemblance to her highborn father, who denied her to his grave. Her mother was a fair-haired kitchen wench with eyes that changed their color to match the lighting of the room, or to match the fires kindling within her soul. Maisie Sessile was naïve enough in those early days to believe his impassioned whispers, and warm-loined enough to convince herself that their tryst was fueled by love rather than his base desire to rut.

The flames were extinguished almost as quickly as they caught. Clemenceau, the baron himself, tromped through the kitchen after a hunt to grab a piece of marchpane. He found the girl alone, but knew others would be bustling back through the kitchen soon enough. He smelled of sweat, leather, and horse. His odor wafted through the kitchen, overpowering the honey cakes that were baking by the fire. Maisie lifted her eyes as she rose from basting the honey cakes. A wisp of flaxen hair escaped her cooking cap and hung languorously before her eye. Clemenceau took three long strides toward her, but she did not cower or drop her gaze as she had been taught to do. The lord would probably strike her for her insolence, but she was frozen. It was as if time held its breath for the next moment.

He lifted his hand and still she did not flinch. Clemenceau popped the marchpane into his mouth, licking the sugar off his finger, and then he took the wisp of hair, running the length of it between his dampened fingers and tucked it behind her ear.

"Comment t'appelles-tu?" he asked, and when she didn't respond immediately repeated, "What are you called?" in a tongue he thought she'd comprehend.

"Maisie, milord," she responded in a voice as honeyed as the basting mop dripping from her hand.

She glanced around the kitchen for signs of others. Why was no one else in the kitchen?

He moved his hand from her ear to her waist and commanded, "Walk with me, Maisie, honey hair."

His grip was strong, and she could feel the heat of his hand through her thin gown. She wore nothing beneath it on the days she was assigned to the baking, for the fire was hot, even in the dead of winter. She walked as commanded, ushered by the lord's hand, his smell permeating her nostrils and intoxicating her with an odd mixture of lust and fear. She suspected what the lord had in mind and knew it would be death to stop it, so she might as well enjoy the tumble.

They entered the mill room, dimly lit by high windows shooting shafts of light at sharp angles onto the neatly stacked sacks of flour.

"Out," Clemenceau commanded the miller seated at his grindstone.

"Yes, my lord," obeyed the miller while casting an accusatory look at Maisie. Word that she had bewitched the lord would be all over the kitchens by this time tomorrow, whether they turned out to be true or not. Clemenceau shut the door behind him, and he spun her into the center of the room while he dropped the wooden lever that bolted the door. He shrugged off his fur, sending the scent of horse and man into the air. Flour dust rose in response.

"Now, Mademoiselle, show me your honeyed locks."

"Milord, your lady wife—" she began, refusing to lower her eyes.

"Is as cold as this winter's day," he finished. He stepped closer. She held her ground.

"Why do you show no fear?" he asked, unaware of the trembling in her veins. She had no escape. He held her at his whim.

"Because I fear you not, milord," she lied and tossed her cooking cap onto a pile of flour sacks. He chuckled.

"Brave words from a lassie I can set beyond the gates whenever I tire of her." He had recaptured her waist, pulling her against him, so she could feel his hardness.

"But, milord, why should you ever tire of me?" she asked as she reached up and pulled her hair from its knot. The hair cascaded down, down, down brushing her thighs as she shook it out. She leaned back a bit so that it would fall behind her shoulders, the light fabric of her cooking shift betraying hardened nipples. Her hair was not really golden but took on golden tones in the shafts of light and in the puffs of flour eddying in the air currents. Her eyes sparked blue in the chill of the room.

In one swift motion, he lifted the shift from her body, tossing it to the floor. She slipped out of her clogs and stood naked before him, a tendril of straight hair cascading over one breast. The angled light illuminated it, and without another word, Clemenceau brushed the tendril aside and bent to her breast, teasing the nipple with a practiced tongue.

His right hand cupped her breast, squeezing gently while his left hand traced the curvature of rib cage and rested shortly in the indentation of her hip. His teeth nipped at her breast with a force that was not quite pleasure, not quite pain. His hand glanced over her buttocks, pulling her close yet again to his codpiece. His lips traveled upward to her throat. He unexpectedly brought her chin in his hand.

"Open your eyes," he growled.

She obeyed, meeting his gaze measure for measure. He took her hand, which had somehow become entangled in his

99

thick, ebony hair, and held it before her. Slowly, painstakingly, he put two of her fingers into his mouth, sucking on them. She closed her eyes in the pleasure of it.

"I said open your eyes. I want to see your face."

He held her hand in his, tracing her own fingers downward over her nipple. With a slight shift, he moved her hand down her stomach and onto her womanhood. His finger bent around hers and guided them inside her with enough force to hurt her wrist. Her eyes widened, and he recognized her pain as he forced her maidenhead with her own hand.

"Ahh," he said. "I am pleasantly surprised. I would expect a girl of your looks to have already been sullied. How fortunate for us both. He had clamped her hand against herself, his finger plying about as she wriggled, an odd warmth surrounding her hand and radiating from her most private of areas. He still held her chin with his other hand, reading her eyes. He released her all at once, and she stumbled backward, suddenly embarrassed at the blood on her hand and between her legs.

"May I see you, milord?" she asked.

"Not today, *mon petite maison*," he replied, and he turned on his heel and unbolted the door. He left her standing naked in the mill room in a fog of flour dust, sullied but not taken. He had awakened a desire within her that would smolder until the next time he came looking for a bit of marchpane.

He took her the very next day in a darkened corridor between a hulking chifferobe and the corner, not ten feet from his lady wife's chambers. Had the walls not been of stone, she might have heard him rutting against Maisie as he lifted her off her feet, all the while holding her by the scruff of the neck, his eyes thrusting into hers in rhythm with his manhood. He was finished almost before he had started; she was not even disheveled.

"There's a good girl," he said, tucking himself back into his pantaloons. He patted her on the head and sent her on her way with a swat to her rump as if she were an obedient little pup.

100

It did not suit Clemenceau that his new plaything was but a kitchen wench, so he had her reassigned as a lady's maid. He wanted her bathed and at the ready. He also took pleasure in seeing his wife sitting in ignorance beside her. Of course, he could do as he pleased with impunity, but it would not do to recklessly flaunt his dalliance right in front of his wife if she were aware of it. As for the girl, she played her part well, never once giving him that fervent glance of hers when she was in the same room as his wife, but she served him his marchpane and much more each evening with a fervency that bespoke of love, and love could be dangerous. Love could make women make stupid decisions, especially an elevated kitchen wench who thought he was falling in love with her.

He often made his way to his lady's chambers afterwards, Maisie's scent still on him, but his wife only flinched and performed her duty with an air of disdain. It smacked of ritual, or a chore, this business of getting a child. He would leave her kneeling at her *prie-dieu*, beseeching God for the son that would put an end to her nightly trials. She was a young wife and would go to her grave knowing nothing of the pleasures of love.

The two became pregnant at once. When Maisie failed to produce a husband, Lady Clemenceau dismissed her without a second thought, and without an inkling of Lord Clemenceau's role. She was turned out to the estate gates. Lady Clemenceau, who was reveling in her own holy pregnancy could not abide a tainted woman in her presence. Her prayers had been answered, and she alone would bask in the glory of an heir. There was no room for any other woman to share in her experience.

This created a problem for Lord Clemenceau, who despite himself, had become quite accustomed to his marchpane. He had yet to satisfy his sweet tooth, and he was a man used to getting his way. He had Maisie intercepted and deposited at an inn he frequented a half-day's ride from the manor. Lady Clemenceau was blissfully unaware of its existence. A gold sovereign ensured Maisie's safekeeping and vouchsafe she would remain untouched, yet held at the pleasure of his orders. The sumptuous room and the servants who provided for her needs left no question that this was her best option. He knew she would be agreeable. After all, what choice had she? If she gave birth to a bastard son, it could be valuable to him. It was a winsome scenario for him. He could keep her at arms' length, pleasure himself when it suited him, and do away with her easily enough when this lovely carriage ride came to a halt. In the meantime, his lady wife would be enraptured by the promise of motherhood. He had another sovereign that would buy the priest's advice suggesting she lie not with her husband while she was with child, a piece of advice that would earn her quick and ready agreement. What fortune! Lord Clemenceau predicted a fine hunting season both before and after her confinement. He was a fortunate man, indeed.

17

Maisie had gotten pregnant despite every precaution—except the obvious one—she had been able to glean from the wise women in the kitchens or even the wizened old crone who served as the midwife to the gentle ladies. Hot possets and vinegar swabs had failed. The stone amulet she wore on a leather thong about her neck was a useless rock. Lord Clemenceau had taken her in ways she had never imagined and had taught her methods for pleasuring a man that could make sensation radiate through herself as well. She had come to love him and thought he must love her in turn since he so often called for her. His treatment of her had to be distant in the presence of her lady. She understood this.

But the pregnancy had almost undone her; she knew she could be tossed away at his whim, left standing alone, naked, and wanting in a cold granary. She wanted to possess him the way he possessed her. She wanted to have power over him in some small way. She did not want to remain merely a plaything, however cherished he claimed her to be through his whispers tainted with sweetmeats.

She would not be owned without taking something in return. She would be paid for her loyalty and for her silence. He had failed to see that her will would not be ignored. She may have been a kitchen wench, but she was no whore. It did not occur to her that whoring was precisely what she had been doing. And now, with a bastard growing within her, sickening her every morning, she had to build a future for them both. She refused to birth a whoreson, and she had plenty of time to draw forth her plot.

Maisie spent her days gazing at the oak leaves outside the upstairs window where she was kept for her confinement. Her condition was obvious now, and she would remain locked away in the rented room until her lying in was well past. The days dragged on without end, the only company being the briefest of minutes when a serving girl would knock at the door with a tray of breakfast or supper. Although the apartment was well-appointed, with a small sitting room and a boudoir, Maisie recognized that her confinement was as much out of Clemenceau's necessity as it was hers. Through the bars of the window, she could just reach the branches of the oak. She marked the days of her confinement by plucking an acorn to signify the passing of each incessant day. Maisie waited, and feeling the child roll in her womb, bided her time.

She received no luncheon and learned soon enough to stow away a roll or apple to feed the child growing within her. A chambermaid visited each morning, wordlessly thrusting an empty pot at Maisie in exchange for the soiled one, while a small boy with a face full of freckles and hair the color of a carrot lit her fire and lay in the day's ration of logs. Saturday mornings brought a trio of men carrying a copper washtub followed by the chambermaid and a pair of identical little girls who were destined to become the crown jewels of a nearby brothel, all lugging copper pails of steaming water. The twin girls scrubbed Maisie clean before twisting her dampened hair into a tight coil at the nape of her neck.

Maisie tried to engage the servants in conversation, to ask for tidbits of news from L'Arbol, Clemenceau's estate, or even the price of butter in the market, but she failed to get them beyond *ouis* and *nons*. She was effectively sequestered. Without the ability to read or to write, she had no contact with the outside world, not that she had anyone aside from the lord himself to contact.

Her cue that Clemenceau was coming was the appearance of a tray of marchpane. She took the opportunity to uncoil her hair, which fell in undulating waves of faded honey. Pregnancy had increased the thickness of her hair, but the lack of exposure to the clear air and natural light erased the streaks of sunshine from it. Pregnancy had also created a fullness in her breasts that Clemenceau was sure to appreciate, not to mention the heady swell of his seed in her womb.

Even in the dimness of the room, her beauty was radiant, and it was on this radiance that she would stake her claim. She took a few turns about the room, as she did every day, to feel the blood course through her veins and bring her color to a rosy pink.

She heard him tromping up the stairs as he approached her room, and she rose, standing in front of the brazier so her appearance would glow all the more when her lord arrived.

A servant opened the door for him, bowing his way aside in response to the gruff "Leave us" intoned by Clemenceau. She stood erect. If anything, she lifted her chin. She most decisively did not lower her gaze.

Clemenceau surveyed her from across the room. She was a haughty wench if ever he saw one, but she was hale, unlike his wife, whom he'd left abed yet another day, her confinement looming for months ahead. Let her stay there. As long as she produced a son, an heir, she could die there for all he cared.

"My lord," she said.

"Mon petite maison," he replied.

He was already unlacing his breeches before she could say more.

***

Afterward, he lay beside her, her hair spread over his chest like a blanket, munching almost daintily on his beloved marchpane.

Clemenceau wrapped a lock of hair around his finger. "It appears you are enjoying your confinement. I trust your needs have been attended?"

"Of course, milord, but I become lonely with only the babe inside for company. I don't even have a *prie-dieu* to pray or even a bit of needlework to occupy my hands. I will need to have my dress let out before much longer. I can do it, milord, if I have needle and thread. I talk to the child lest I turn to despair." Maisie kept her voice even. He would broach no begging.

"I will not have you despairing, *mon amour,*" he said tenderly. "I am occupied with my holdings and have not thought beyond the basics of keeping you, *petite jeté.* This cage protects you and the child from prying eyes, from ignominy. It keeps you within my reach." He moved from her hair back to her breast. "What do you say?" he asked as his lips brushed the growing bump on her stomach.

"To your son, milord? Why, I tell him his name, of course. I whisper Clemenceau, Randall Clemenceau," she replied.

The slap was not unexpected, but it came hard, stinging her cheek and drawing blood from her lip.

"My lord?" she asked, eyes never leaving his, not even in her pain.

"Only I can grant him that name. It is not yours to give. How do I even know he comes from my seed?"

Her voice dropped low and icy, both respectful and repulsed. "Because you're the only man who has shared my bed, milord." Her *milord* had venom in it.

He shot back, "You weren't even a maid when I took you, wench, and you would do well to remember that."

"You know you took my maidenhead, lord. Yes, it was by my hand, but you guided it. You would do well to remember that."

This time his fist was closed when it came across her cheek. "You forget your place, *mon fête.*"

He rose from her bed, leaving her holding her head in her hands, droplets of blood staining the hair that had flown across her face with the impact of the blow.

"I will return when you've learned it. I advise you to bear a son, or you'll be reduced to nothing more than a cast-off whore." He strode from the room, calling for his groom.

Nevertheless, a *prie-dieu,* basket of needlework, and a brocade gown appeared the next week. Along with the gown came a tiny wooden cask. Inside the cask was a pair of bone hair combs, polished to an opalescent sheen, and a silvered beaten rattle. After inspecting these curious gifts, Maisie deduced that the health of the legitimate heir and his mother must be in question. She put the *prie-dieu* to excellent use that evening, praying fervently for the death of Lady Clemenceau.

18

By the time the tray of marchpane appeared again in Maisie's chamber, the bruise on her cheekbone had faded to gray-green. She was nearing her term, but her largesse did not deter Clemenceau's need to satisfy himself.

"Your lying-in should commence soon," he said. "I shall send the midwife to you when your pains begin."

"Thank you, my lord," she kept her eyes and tone respectful, mostly out of fear that he might inadvertently harm the child, for she was close to her time indeed.

"Where shall I go to raise the child?" she asked calmly, for surely he did not intend to confine both her and their baby in this chamber indefinitely.

"Back to L'Arbol, of course," he responded.

"But, Lady Clemenceau turned me out, my lord."

"And I shall turn you back in again, *mon chéri*. I wish to hold you still. You shall have a place in the nursery."

The idea of feeding Lady Clemenceau's mewling and puking child while her own baby had to wait repulsed her but would afford her the perfect opportunity to put her ploy into motion. She could not have planned it better herself. Her son would bear the Clemenceau name. She was sure of it.

"You will be near enough for this whenever I please," he said as he pushed her head into his lap. She knew precisely what to do, veritably attacking his groin with urgent determination. His groan moments later was all the signal she needed. She had him.

***

Lady Clemenceau and Maisie went into their respective labors on the same winter day, but that was where the parallels came to an abrupt end. Maisie's labor was easy by the standards of child-bearing. The midwife would not have had time to make the half-day ride to the inn even if she weren't occupied with Lady Clemenceau's strident screams.

Yet, Maisie's inexperience and the shocked faces of the twin serving girls lent credence to her fears, and she cried out a stream of curses as the baby's head crowned and stopped dead in her passageway. Pierre, the boy who lit her fire each morning, had been swathing her forehead with a cool vinegar cloth, when he ran crying from the room. A boy had no place in a birthing room, even if he did attend the hearth.

She pushed again to no avail. The chambermaid stepped forward, reaching between Maisie's straining legs. Maisie was too busy cursing and screaming to notice the knife that deftly loosened her grip on the baby's head. The shoulder slipped out on her next push, and the chambermaid delivered the wriggling, pink baby, already protesting its passage into this new, cold world.

Exhaustion set in at that point as the chambermaid put the swaddled infant to Maisie's breast. The baby rooted about, finally getting a purchase on the nipple, sucking noisily.

"My son," Maisie crooned.

"Non, mademoiselle," whispered the chambermaid, looking quickly about the room for curious ears, *"C'est une fille."*

Lord Rene Clemenceau paced his way across the library chamber during the interminably long hours of Camille's labor. He had braced the fire himself, even tossing in a couple of his grandfather's old books because the smell of burning leather settled his nerves. What were they but words? Words could be replaced with relative ease.

Clemenceau was not a collector of words, but he was a connoisseur of wines. He'd much rather invest his fortune in vintages than vellum, but a manor wasn't a true manor without a sizeable library, so he only placated to his book-burning fancy in those hours where his future seemed in question.

He had already nibbled an entire tray of marchpane by the time the priest entered the library with the healer hard on his heels. His sweet tooth fueled his desire. At the moment, his desire was for his heir to finish the business of being born so that he could begin his business of solidifying the Clemenceau fortune, which had dwindled considerably under his tutelage.

"My Lord Rene," began the priest, proffering his hand. *Frère* Jacobi was the only man who called Clemenceau by his Christian name. He rarely even thought of himself as Rene. He felt the name denoted weakness and generally avoided it, rebuffing its use even by Camille, especially by Camille. She had tried it out on her tongue when she had first come to L'Arbol, sitting in the solarium amongst the maids he had placed to be her companions. The name came out trippingly enough but not as quickly as the back of his hand. She never dared call him by his given name again. He would ever be My Lord Clemenceau.

Now she was grunting in her chambers above, closed off while she did her woman's work. She would give him his heir. She would give him his future. Her simpering, cold looks were a low enough price to pay. He could tuck her away easily enough within the walls of L'Arbol, only seeing her on those occasions he felt it necessary to get another heir. She had strong bloodlines and would serve him well.

"*Frère Jacobi*, does my lady wife bring forth a son?"

"Not yet, milord, these things take patience. Some women labor for well over a day before their ordeal draws to a happy close," the priest replied.

"Lord, Lady Camille calls for you," said the healer. "Her way is particularly difficult. I advise you to offer her some comfort."

"I'll offer her comfort when she produces my son," Clemenceau responded harshly. "I can't stomach her whines and screams. It can't possibly be that bad. Lesser women have squatted in the fields with nary a whimper."

"My Lord, she gives you your heir," *Frère* Jacobi rebuked him as sternly as he dared.

Clemenceau softened. "Yes, *Frère.* That she does. But, still, I shall not move to her side until the babe is in arms." He poured a cup of claret whose sweetness cloyed against the sweetness of the marchpane. He handed it to the healer.

"Take this wine to fortify her, Master Henri, as a gift from her lord."

"Yes, my lord. I have already ordered the kitchens to prepare lamb's marrow for strength. It is a tedious business, this first child."

"Would the Father bless you with many sons," added the priest.

"Amen," finished Master Henri as he and *Frère* Jacobi backed their way out of the library and scurried up the stairs to continue their business. Both men were well aware that there would be hell to pay if the Father did not bestow His blessing upon Clemenceau. They were both lost in silent prayer as they climbed the stairs to the struggling lady's room, which was kept roasting hot to warm the babe as it made its way into the world.

Clemenceau plopped into a boar's hair chair before the blazing fire. "I don't need the many; I just need the one," he said to the flames as they licked the pages of the smoldering book as if the words were sweetmeats themselves. He felt secure in the knowledge that his bastard son would be waiting in the wings.

Lady Camille thrashed in agony, ever weakening from the pains that wracked her body and the blood that flowed between

111

her legs. The child refused to come. *Frère* Jacobi prayed over her, even placed a rosary into her hands, but it was to no avail. Master Henri applied a lamb's marrow poultice to her mountainous belly, but it did not encourage the child. The midwife was summoned when the men reached the end of their birthing expertise, standing helplessly by as Lady Camille strained, producing nothing but a steady trickle of blood.

It was hot, so very hot in the room, like the height of summer. For a few moments, her head swam, and she saw her own lady mother peering at her adoringly as she lay in her cradle, but the contractions brought her back to agonizing reality. She needed help. She was being ripped apart by her son, who would probably be as cruel as his father. Clemenceau would make certain of that. She had flung the wine from the healer's hand, the flagon bouncing off the oaken floor. Surely, childbirth was not supposed to be this difficult. Something was wrong. She bellowed and pulled at the sheets as the next wave of pain wracked her body.

The midwife arrived at last. She assisted the servants and plainfolk with their birthings, husbands or not, and in rare situations, she assisted the mares in the stables. Her stench preceded her, as she believed bathing in the winter would cause the death fevers, but she at least had the good grace to dunk her hands into the water bowl before beginning her work.

"Open the windows, all of them, *Frère*. It's like the mouth of Hell in here," she ordered.

"She'll catch her death from the cold," he protested.

"It may already have a hold. She is weak. I need to look to the babe. Girl, bring forth that light."

The priest nodded to a serving girl kneeling in a corner who handed him a candle and went to opening windows. The chill winter air blew in immediately, exchanging itself with the stifling heat.

"Go to her head, healer, swab her with cooling cloths. She is feverish, can't you see?" The midwife spoke sharply to the

112

men, more sharply than any woman had right, but her words to Camille were bathed in gentleness.

"I will help you, child. I will help your baby. You must ride the pain. Do not fight against it. Breathe the cool air and plow through the pains like a ship plowing through the swells. Yes, the waves batter, but your ship is sure. Your ship is sure, Lady."

Somehow, the midwife's words calmed Camille enough for the panic to leave her eyes before the next pains came. The midwife was at the ready and moved her hand into the womb to get a purchase on the child.

"I must turn your baby, Lady. That is why he cannot come."

The midwife did not wait for acknowledgement of permission but proceeded to press down on Camille's belly while she screamed. The last thing Camille remembered was a ripping and blood, so much blood.

"Priest, you'd do well to call on your god now. The baby is stuck fast. Henri, please go bid our lord his druthers. He may have a wife or a child. I shan't be able to save them both. Hurry, there isn't much time. We could lose them both."

She cooed softly as she worked, Camille drifting in and out of consciousness as time wore on. At length, the healer returned.

"Milord says our heads shall decorate the gates of L'Arbol if his son falls. He ordered his groom to saddle his hunter. The lord says he is dreadfully bored with the whole business. The lady, he insists, is expendable." Mercifully, she was unable to hear her husband's pronouncement. The midwife nodded, acknowledging the task before her.

"Prepare this in mulled wine and give it to her. Force it down if need be," she said handing a posset to Henri. "It will at least ease her path as I do what I must."

The child was born in a pool of blood and put to suckle as Camille's strength drained slowly but without relief. The midwife could not stem the bleeding, even with cobweb packings. The baby cried plaintively, remorsefully, for the sin of killing her mother, and for the sin of being born a girl when her father clearly demanded a son.

He rode hard as if by galloping he could knit up the plans that were coming unraveled before him. Camille was failing him as he suspected she would. Maisie had the stubbornness to withstand the pains of childbirth and would likely be with child again within a fortnight of resumed whoring. He found it ironic that the cultured, high-born wife was the physical weakling while the nameless kitchen wench was hale. Either way, they would both provide him a son. Of this, he was certain. He rode to meet his new son, although he'd never give him his name. The boy would prove much more useful as a bastard than as a coddled lordling. Maisie was so lovely, he would bring her back as nursemaid to his true son. Perhaps he would suck some of the strength of will that his mother lacked. She could warm his bed as well. A half-day's ride was a high fee even for the goods Maisie so willingly offered. Clemenceau relished the idea that he could have both women so easily in his thrall. Both had distinct treasures to offer, one bought for her blood, the other for her silence.

The hunter was well-lathered, and Clemenceau's arse ached in the saddle by the time he arrived at the inn. Would there had been another place nearer to the chateau, but this place asked no questions about the imprisoned woman and guarded her well. Why, she didn't even truly realize she had been caged. No matter. He could replace her for a farthing and a smile when he grew weary of her. He just wasn't tired of her, yet. She would be a ripe, juicy plum for the picking within a few weeks. His loins stirred just thinking about it. He grew hard when he thought of his unsuspecting lady wife cooing over Maisie's son. The priest would lead her to forgive Maisie's un-handfasted dalliance, and she would welcome the girl who would suckle the boys, secret brothers, side by side. Everyone could be bought. Everyone could be sold. The trick was knowing which secrets to make known and which secrets to hold.

He took the stairs of the inn two at a time when he heard the baby's crying. Maisie was resplendent in the winter afternoon light, casting golds, bronzes, and silvers through her hair, which graced her shoulder in a thin braid that seemed to go on for miles. A bald head was sucking noisily at her breast, the other exposed and full, its nipple reflecting the light in the droplets of mother's milk that had risen.

"How now, *mon petite maison.* How fares my son?"

Hesitation flashed in her eyes, but then she drew up her chin. "Your son is no son at all, milord, but a fair-eyed baby girl." She dared not ask for his name, but added, "I have yet to name her."

"You disappoint me, Maisie. I expected a strapping son, not this balded *fille.* Let me see."

Maisie plucked the baby from her breast and held her out for Clemenceau's inspection. The baby's eyes were fair but shifted from icy blue to green as he turned her in the light. The child had Maisie's eyes set in a miniature of his features. Her patronage would be unmistakable, perhaps even to Camille's naïve mind.

He briefly envisioned dashing the babe's head against the stone fireplace and having done with it but handed the child gently back to its mother. This girl would grow to be a great beauty. Perhaps there would be value in that.

"I must ride back to the chateau to greet my son who shall have been born by the time I arrive. You shall quit your chambers here immediately, *mon chéri.*"

Her eyes widened. Was he casting her aside, along with his daughter? "My lord, have pity…" She knew he had no mercy. "My lying-in. I must heal."

"And heal you shall, at L'Arbol. You will serve as nursemaid for my son and warm my bed soon enough. A cart shall gather you on the morrow. Lie on bedding if you must, but come tomorrow you shall return to L'Arbol.

"What of the babe?"

"Bring her. Name her as you will as long as she does not bear the name Clemenceau. That is a name you shall not hold. You are but a whore, a beautiful whore, but a whore nonetheless. If you want this little one to rise above your station, you'll keep your tongue well in check."

"Yes, milord, but my tongue and all of its talents must be rewarded for exercising such silence," she countered.

"You forget yourself. Your tongue can be cut out of that pretty little mouth at my command."

She licked her lower lip seductively. "But you'd never want to do that, would you, my lord?"

He chuckled. "You speak true. You'd best hope I don't find another plaything and keep your insolent tongue as a souvenir in a jar. I shall call on you again in L'Arbol," he said and shut the door on mother and baby, chuckling all the while.

He took bread and a hearty venison stew before leaving the inn. He also took both of the twin girls, right there at the table. They were a little young for his taste, but both had been plucked before. They rode his lap in turns as he casually downed a frothy ale. When he had drunk his fill, he swept the leavings off the table and bent them over it, side by side, lifting their skirts, and riding them both with a ferocity that surprised even him. They whimpered, whether in agony or ecstasy, he did not know or care, as he gripped their hips, grinding them together as if they were one. When he was finished, he tossed two coins on the table.

Glancing around at his guards, who had been stationed at the inn to ensure Maisie's silence, he slapped the twins on their exposed arses. "A double reward for a job well done, men," he said heartily.

He tossed another coin to the innkeeper, who was as like their father as not. "Join in if you'd like," he laughed, taking his

116

leave as his four hired men queued up for their turns to bid farewell to the remote inn.

Upstairs, Maisie lay oblivious to the raucous behavior below. She was mesmerized by the beauty of the child in her arms and whispered blessings on her head.

"He will recognize you, my darling. He will not toss you away. I will vouchsafe your way, my beautiful, beautiful Renae."

19

Clemenceau's ire when he discovered he had been doubly jilted of an heir, on the same day no less, was great. Furthermore, his wife lay stone dead, having at last bled out in her efforts to bear him a son. The only blessing for her was that she did not regain consciousness after the midwife's grisly work and so went to her Catholic God unaware it had all been for nothing.

He looked at the swaddled girl, bald and blue-eyed. The baby looked very much like the baby he had left hours earlier. But then, all babies look similar when they are newborn.

In his anger, or in his grief as the story was later told, he drew his rapier and slew Master Henri where he stood, running him through, pinning him against the great oaken headboard like a butterfly in one of the curiosity boxes in the solarium.

As the life left Henri's eyes, he muttered a garbled "Why?"

To this Clemenceau hissed, "Why ever not?" and tugged the rapier from the healer's chest. Henri sank to the bed, covering Camille's head with his bleeding body. The reeking midwife ran bellowing from the scene, the newborn safe in her grasp.

Clemenceau's guardsmen burst in and grabbed their lord then, to protect him from his own distraught grief. With his arms pinned to his sides, they manhandled him back to his library, and the priest was summoned to calm him and absolve him for his impulsive act. None seemed too concerned about the fate of the healer. He was just an unfortunate fool who had been at the wrong place when the lord met with his grief.

A dead wife was a tragedy whether she was treasured or not by the husband. A dead lady wife spelled change for the servants. It marked a time when they must look to themselves before another lady emerged to take the helm, another lady who may have vastly different requirements and expectations from the one who preceded her. It would be an eggshell season for the housekeepers of L'Arbol. Surely, the lord would seek another wife with haste. After all, he still needed an heir.

This proved to be an eggshell season for Maisie as well. She nursed both Renny and the motherless Elyse, who grew strong. It was as widely known throughout L'Arbol that she shared Lord Clemenceau's bed as it was that she was just a kitchen wench, stirring pots a year ago. Yet, he dressed her in spring silks and granted her attendants. She ordered entertainments and commissioned dresses for the babies, whom she clothed in lace with no differentiation between the highborn girl and the baseborn girl. In the nursery of L'Arbol, they were equals, and the nursery encompassed their whole world.

He allowed her to persist in this fantasy, because it amused him, a pretty whore playing at living dolls. She was vilified in the kitchens and stables alike. Burrs would be overlooked by the saddler if she called for the palfrey Clemenceau had gifted her with. Spittle was a staple ingredient in foods served to the nursery. Lord Clemenceau appeared besotted with her, and they hated her for it. As long as she stood in the way, a new lady for L'Arbol would not be found. An heir would not grace the courtyards of the chateau.

In truth, Lord Clemenceau was besotted with Maisie. Inch by inch, caress by caress, she had gentled him into complacency. He knew he must find a new bride, one with the correct bloodlines to align with the Clemenceau name, but there would be plenty of time for that. Let him take a young bride in his middle age. He could get an heir on her and enjoy the pleasures of Maisie in the meantime while his virility was at its peak.

As the little daughters grew into their toddlerhood, they began to distinguish themselves from one another. Elyse had thick, tight curls like her dead mother but called Maisie *Maman*. She was unmistakably his child, stocky in stature with a chin favoring strength over beauty. One had to look carefully to see his seed in Renny, who so closely resembled Maisie that his likeness was lost on her at a casual glance. But he was there in her demeanor and in her eyes that changed color when the light shifted. They were her mother's eyes, but Renny had a quality about hers that set his teeth on edge. The child's eyes spooked him. They were calculating, piercing eyes seeming to have the capacity to read into his soul. They bulged from her head, playing into the perception she could see with a vision very few possess. Gossamer hair grew willy-nilly on her head, looking for all the world like spun sugar. It was straight like her mother's, but instead of cascading in a waterfall hugging the shape of her head, Renny's hair stood on end, reaching for the crackling fire in the grate. She had a singularly off-putting appearance.

Time began to slide forward. A slippery slope of hunting, whoring, and feasting managed to keep Clemenceau's temper in check. He ignored the priest and would have dismissed him long ago had the holy man not kept the servants in check with his fearmongering. Clemenceau did as he pleased at L'Arbol with impunity, as was his birthright. He had his way with most of the serving maids and even a few of the apprentice grooms with varying degrees of ferocity, but not forcibly, for they all submitted readily enough. His appetite was great and varied. A turn of a skirt or a reflection of a buckle could set him off, and he was not a man to be denied.

Yet Maisie hung on, relentlessly insinuating herself in the business of L'Arbol, positioning Renny favorably while pushing Elyse almost imperceptibly to the side. She taught herself to read in those long nursery hours and listened intently at her sampler while the girls took their ciphering lessons. Both girls were to be educated; she had insisted in her sidestepping persistence, and Clemenceau capitulated. Renny clearly had an aptitude for learning that Elyse simply did not possess. Her ineptitude would make her all the more pliable when the time came.

Clemenceau knew Maisie was positioning her daughter and watched with amusement while she elevated herself on a house of cards. He was impressed with her almost imperceptible scheming, but it was, after all, almost imperceptible. Had he been in her position, he would have been grasping in the same way. He respected her for that, if respect was the right word for it. He had a few surprises in mind for his beautiful little whore, which he knew she would not find to her liking.

Each night, in the wee hours of darkness, Maisie crept back to the nursery and crawled into the bed with Renny. Renny's warm little body lulled her back toward slumber as she whispered into the sleeping child's ear.

"You are valuable, Renny, no matter what happens. You are a treasure, and you must fight for what is yours. It is your name, Renny. You must fight for your name, or if you cannot have it, you must keep it from the hands of others. You are Clemenceau, and you will have your legacy. You are Clemenceau here in the night, although we cannot say it in the light of day. L'Arbol shall be yours. L'Arbol shall be yours."

The child would stir and mouth, *"Oui, Mama. Je suis Clemenceau. Je suis votre arbre vivant."* She never made mention of the nighttime ritual in the day, but Renny's eyes had knowledge behind them. Maisie imagined her future might not have happiness, but Renny would have her name. She would have her legacy.

20

She arrived at L'Arbol amidst great fanfare. The servants lined the cobbled entrance with Maisie at their head, visibly swallowing her pride. Maisie had been summoned to the library less than an hour before and told succinctly that her services as nursemaid were no longer required. She was to present Elyse, along with the keys to the spice cupboard, to his new bride—he had been wed hastily to the fifteen-year-old daughter of a viscount on his last hunting expedition—and step into the background. If she left quietly, she and her daughter would be afforded the luxury of her former quarters in the inn a half-day's ride away. She would afford him the luxury of her bed when he hunted, which she knew was often.

"And if I refuse?" she asked icily, taken aback. She knew the day would come when he would toss her aside and had been vigilant for signs of his waning passion. There were none. In fact, she had warmed his bed the previous evening. The man's duplicity was unfathomable. His demeanor could move from caring to cruel in the time between chimes as the clock struck the hour. She thought she had made herself valuable to him. She even suspected he loved her, but it was a cruel love that set another, and his own child as well, on a shelf to have a different woman out. But he had done it before. He had done it with her. Why should she be immune to his caprice? The coffers must be emptying even more quickly than was whispered by the priest, between squeaky little gasps, trading Clemenceau's confessions for her mouth on his cock.

"If you refuse? Why, *mon chéri,* I will cry and claim to my lovely young wife that I have been bewitched by a whore. She shall put you out, and there will be no one to help you this time. Everyone at L'Arbol will turn their backs on you to a person. The women will do worse. You've ensured that yourself, and don't think you can turn to the priest for absolution. I've seen your confessions with mine own eyes."

Damn. The priest had played her false. She thought of Renny, whose future she had been working to secure as Clemenceau was securing his own. It was as if he read her mind.

"Refuse me, and your precious Renny shall meet with an unfortunate end within the hour. I have but to ring this bell, and my man will toss her from the banister. He stands at the ready at her door this very moment. She will break her neck. Not from the fall, of course, but that is how it shall appear. It would be a pity. She will make a fine whore one day, like her mother before her."

"She is your own child," Maisie hissed.

"I have not claimed her, and I never shall. She is nothing to me. You are nothing to me," he said as he toyed with the bell. It was heady, really, holding the power of life and death in his hand. A tinny peal would rid him of both in a single swipe, but he did not ring the bell. He knew if he did, Maisie would fly at him, and he would have no recourse but to run her through. He would hate to spill blood on his new deerskin rug.

"Please, my lord. Leave her. She is your blood whether you claim her or not; I swear it." Maisie lowered her eyes, and he knew she was utterly defeated. It was a delicious sensation, watching her break.

"I beg you, do not harm my daughter, sir. At least show that much pity if you have it not in you to show mercy. Do with me what you will." Her voice was meek with no hint of the haughtiness he had found attractive these many years. He was reminded of his first wife, Camille. He spat upon his prized deerskin rug to ward off her spirit.

"I already have, *mon petite maison*, and evermore shall I continue." He clamped the bell forcefully onto the desktop, where it clanged, but not resoundingly. Maisie flinched. It was the most arousing thing she'd done in months. He would like to see that flinch again. Yes, he would return his little bird to her cage and use the daughter as leverage. She would be agreeable enough when he made the girl flinch. She would be agreeable now. A mother's love was such a predictable thing it nearly brought him to a state of ennui.

"Now that we understand one another, Maisie, you will prepare my daughter to meet her new mother. Little Renny will be kept in your chambers until you have performed your duty. You will find her much changed, a little contract for your cooperation, my dear." He leaned back in the chair, clearly enjoying her agony. He ran his finger along the curvature of the bell, lifting it again to flick the clapper against his knuckle. He could not contain his smile.

"You can leave L'Arbol with your daughter, chin held high, or you can leave L'Arbol alone in chains, known for the whore you are. The choice is entirely up to you."

"You know I will do your bidding. I always have." Maisie dropped to a knee.

"Just like a good whore. I expect a convincing performance." The sound of hooves on cobblestones traveled through the library chimney, an accident of acoustics that kept him abreast of the comings and goings of L'Arbol.

"Our futures await." He lifted her gently and ushered her to the door. She recoiled from his touch, and the gentle hand transformed, shaking her with neck-rattling intensity.

"Why, milord, why?" she begged, defeated.

"Why ever not?" was his only reply.

Maisie rushed up the stairs, trying to make sense of this turning of the tables and grasping desperately to turn them aright again. A guard refused to look at her and stood at the door of her chamber, her wailing child inside. He allowed her to push past him.

Sitting in the middle of the bed was Renny in her dressing gown, her scalp reddened and bleeding in multiple places. Locks of gossamer lay littered on the counterpane around her where her hair had been ripped from her head by a razor. She had struggled against the indignity and had been cut for her efforts. She picked up the hair, placing it on her own head again and again as it fell, wailing "Elyse, Elyse."

"Child. It is only hair. It will grow back," Maisie cried for her Renny, for her forfeited beauty.

"Elyse cut me," Renny said flatly. "They held me down and she cut me. She laughed as she pulled my hair." Renny's eyes took on a far-off quality. Maisie knew she was burning the experience into her memory. It was Renny's first betrayal, and it would not go unpunished.

"Wash your head and find your cloak. We have been turned out. I must attend Elyse a final time, and I will be back to collect you. We will remember this, child. We will remember," Maisie said as she gathered the beloved hair and threw it onto the brazier. The odor of burning hair filled the room and made Renny cry all the more.

"Dry your tears, child. Your hair shall return, but we shall not. I am undone."

"What have you done, *Maman?*" Renny asked, eyes narrowed and accusatory.

"Much more than you shall know, my love. Now find that cloak and wait for me here. Do not leave this room. I will come for you shortly. We are no longer welcome at L'Arbol. Mark me. I will return soon."

Maisie passed through the door that separated the girls' chambers to find Elyse sitting sullenly upon her tufted stool.

125

She looked up at Maisie fearfully, but Maisie's bright voice settled her immediately. She would see no more trouble from her nursemaid, not now or ever again. "Elyse, what a beauty you are with your thick curls! Now, why are you sitting there pouting when the time has come to meet your new *maman*?"

Maisie took the tortoise brush and approached the little girl, gently wrapping her curls around her finger as she prepared her hair.

"You look so lovely, Elyse. Your new *maman* will have no choice but to love you."

"I am lovelier than Renny, am I not, mademoiselle?"

"You know that you are today, my little lady." She tugged calmly at the child's hair, and Elyse prattled.

"Papa says I am the prettiest girl in all the land," she simpered.

"Yes, child," Maisie agreed, mastering her tears for her suffering child in the next room.

"Papa said we needed to teach Renny a lesson. We needed to teach her she will never be as pretty as I am," the child went on, completely ignoring the fact that she was speaking to the mother of the child in need of this cruel education. She saw through those who served her in the same way her father did. Even her nursemaid was nothing more than furniture for her use.

"She's not pretty at all, now, is she?" Elyse smiled into the looking glass as Maisie arranged two curls in front of her shoulder.

"No, not this day," replied Maisie, who would enjoy nothing so much as the pleasure of ripping the curls right out of Elyse's vain little head. The thought of the guard outside the door and the bell sitting on Clemenceau's desk kept her well in check.

"Come now, mademoiselle. Let's hand you to your mother."

126

"Papa says her beauty far exceeds yours. She has dark curls, like mine."

Elyse's bedroom entrance had no post, so they turned the corner unmolested into the hall. Elyse saw the guard at Renny's door and stood before him, pointing a stubby finger toward his face.

"Remember, Ugly Renny must stay in her room. She may not meet my *maman*, for she is too monstrous to be seen."

"Yes, milady," the guard replied, pointedly ignoring Maisie.

Elyse smiled sweetly at Maisie, took her hand, and skipped happily down the corridor. Maisie's smile was already pasted on.

The carriage arrived just as Maisie took her place at the head of the entrance steps. The Lady Adele Clemenceau was handed down by Lord Clemenceau himself. She was small for her age, underdeveloped, and nervous. Maisie doubted the girl had even begun her monthly courses, which would make the immediate production of an heir an impossibility. Her hair was teased into a messy pile on top of her head, a feathered headpiece exaggerating the nest-like effect. On her breast, she wore a ruby pin, the same ruby pin Clemenceau had once given to her. Things had developed so quickly, she hadn't even time to check her jewel coffer, but there was no need now. It was undoubtedly empty.

"Madame, I give you L'Arbol," Lord Clemenceau said gallantly, and the servants opened their arms in the traditional lady's welcome before sweeping their heads low.

Maisie remained erect. The girl, though young, possessed great beauty, perhaps even more than she. Elyse tugged at Maisie's hand, prying herself loose.

"I am Elyse, *Maman*," the girl announced, curls bouncing as she descended the stairs to embrace her father's new wife. "Papa said you were beautiful," Elyse curtsied, a picture of manners.

"And my lord said you were the most beautiful child in all the land," the Lady Adele returned. Elyse smiled triumphantly at her former nursemaid, surreptitiously eying her new mother's bushy hair.

It was Maisie's turn to present the keys to the cupboard, a ritual that marked the official passing of responsibility from one woman to another, most naturally the lady of the house.

Ironically, the keys were traditionally presented on a small plate with a piece of marchpane. The cooks had outdone themselves for this occasion, which apparently all but Maisie knew about, and had shaped the marchpane into a tiny replica of the chateau, down to the placement of the windows flanking the main entrance. Maisie couldn't help but smile a little at the thought of what marchpane was soon to mean for the young Lady Adele. She played her part flawlessly, with no hint of fear or passion. The other servants applauded as Lady Adele held up the molded candy for all to see and took a hearty bite. The servants were applauding Maisie's departure more so than the new bride's arrival, but Maisie persisted with the introductions nevertheless.

She named each servant one by one, taking their hands in hers and giving their hands to the incoming lady of the manor. She couldn't help but notice as she took a servant's hand, the middle and ring fingers were crossed in the sign against witchcraft. So, they truly believed she was a witch. Clemenceau was absolutely right. She had no allies in the kitchens or servants' quarters in L'Arbol. She and Renny were truly alone and would be fortunate to escape unscathed.

Lord Clemenceau watched the quiet dignity of the whore and the anxious embarrassment of the bride. She could hold up the end of a bargain, even in desperation. Renny was an excellent bargaining chip he intended to use repeatedly.

It was not until she had reached the end of the receiving line that Maisie stumbled. There was only one chink in the armor she had drawn up around herself. Her last act as keeper of

128

the house was to clasp the hands of the lord and lady and welcome them to their new life together. She was to offer a blessing. She glanced around for the priest, but, oddly, he was nowhere in sight. Frankly, she was surprised he had missed this show of power. Perhaps he had been overcome by the guilt of his transgressions and elected to pray in the chapel.

Lord Clemenceau had taken his place on the bottom step, the new Lady Clemenceau on the ground level below him. Maisie descended the stairs to reenact their holdfast. From two steps above, she was brought eye to eye with Clemenceau. He held out his hand, crossing his middle and ring fingers with a grin. She caught her breath and took his hand in hers. Six hands were joined together. Lady Clemenceau formed the heart of the tableau, with her hands pressed as if in prayer. Lord Clemenceau placed his hands over hers, in the role of champion protectorate. Maisie rested her thumbs on his hands to form the symbol of a rooftop. Just that slight touch made her blood run cold, and for a moment, she was at a loss for words.

"May the Lord God bless this home, making it fruitful."

At this point, Elyse was fairly bursting with excitement. She danced under Maisie's arms, breaking her physical connection to the couple and thus, spoiling the blessing, but Elyse was too excited to notice her faux pas.

"Papa says you'll give me a baby brother!" she called out to Adele. "When shall I have my brother? Is he here now? Is he in your stomach?"

She skipped around the trio, curls bouncing. Lady Adele laughed out loud. "I'm afraid I don't have a baby brother for you today, little one. I'd prefer to have a little girl just like you!"

"Oui," said Elyse. "You already do! I am here, *ici!"*

Lord Clemenceau laughed as well, but his eyes weren't laughing at all. "I'd prefer to have a little heir, the sooner the better. Come, wife. Enter your new maison."

As he led his new bride and daughter into the chateau, he turned briefly back to Maisie. "I believe you have an appointment, my dear," he said in his most mannerly voice. "I shall ring for you when I require you again."

He turned his attention to his wife. "My dearest Adele, I have a fetching little bell in my library that will have my servants rushing to their duties."

"Papa, may I ring the bell? May I?" sang Elyse.

"Perhaps in a bit, my pet. We don't want to send a false order, now do we?" He looked at Maisie, who was already fleeing up the stairs.

21

It was barely a fortnight before the telltale tray of marchpane was delivered to Maisie's inn chambers. Her pregnancy was no longer an issue, so she and Renny were afforded the luxury of stepping out to the village market. Still, Maisie kept Renny well away from the prying eyes of strangers and would never let her venture out of the chambers unaccompanied.

Two hired men swapped shifts, guarding Lord Clemenceau's treasures, never failing to bar the chamber doors from the outside at dusk each evening. When Maisie would rise at daybreak, a boy would enter to start the day's fire and would leave the door ajar, making it easy to pretend they weren't prisoners. But the hired man would be at his post, usually leaned back against the wall in a chair, carving a wooden figure that he would offer wordlessly to the child.

It was the warmest act of kindness she received from the outside world. All in all, they were largely ignored. She had attempted to gallop away one morning, tossing Renny up on the saddle of a gelding standing ready for another patron of the inn. The horse, however, was difficult to handle, and they were reined in by the stouter guardsman not two miles from the inn.

She was taught a hard lesson that day. Wordlessly, the guardsman escorted them back to the upstairs quarters. Instead of barring the door as she expected, he followed them into the room and pushed her hard into the chair. When she sprang back up, she was met with the back of his gloved hand. The glove was wrapped in chain mail. Pain exploded across her cheek, and she sank into the chair. She must have lost consciousness, for when she opened her eyes, he had Renny lashed to the bedpost, skirts over her head. He beat Renny bloody with a strap against her bare thighs. It was Renny's screams that roused her. When she attempted to rise, her head swam in dazzling lights, and she was powerless. The guardsman untied Renny, laid her gently on the bed, face down, and left the room. He did not speak. He did not need to. The glove and strap had spoken for him.

The door was barred for a month after that, opening only for the fire boy, chambermaid, and innkeeper, who delivered their breakfast and dinner without fail.

When the tray of marchpane appeared, the bruise on Maisie's face was still a kaleidoscope of purples and greens. Doubtless, Lord Clemenceau had received the report of their feeble attempt at escape. She steadied her nerves for the next onslaught.

The upstairs chamber-prison consisted of a sitting room with a bedroom to the rear. It likely had been two separate private rooms at the end of the corridor, possibly even the private rooms for the innkeeper's family.

The twins from her earlier confinement had not appeared in this detention, and her casual inquiry about them was met with the usual silence. The silence was an effective torture in itself. She had Renny to speak to, of course, and they often sang the old songs of gallant knights and chattered throughout the day, but a woman craves conversation with someone other than a child, albeit a bright one.

Healing balms had been added to the supper tray the night of the beating, so Maisie knew there was pity at least, if not concern, for their situation. Maisie had applied the balms, mixed with her own tears, to the child's legs, apologizing for her pain, and promising not to attempt to leave again.

Renny's hair still had not recovered from the shearing, growing back in uneven tufts. She kept it covered in a skullcap, wisps barely peeking out from its laced hem. The beating had a surprising effect on Renny. It made her absolutely determined to escape the inn and the clutches of Lord Clemenceau. The child was willing to risk another beating, if the reward was freedom, but Maisie openly discouraged her talk of such. Maisie knew the beating was merely a warning, and a repeat performance would warrant a much sterner punishment. She could not bear the risk. The child neither understood that nor the risk she faced.

Lord Clemenceau entered the chambers, directing Renny to close herself within. He fingered his marchpane as he examined Maisie's bruised cheek. "This is child's play compared to what you'll both get if you attempt that lunacy again," he said flatly, brushing the cheekbone with the back of his hand just to agitate the bruise and punctuate his meaning.

"Yes, milord," she returned.

"I am to be a father," he said.

"Congratulations," she offered sans sentiment.

"I shall have my son at last."

"That is what you thought before, my lord."

"That was because I was getting a child on a weakling and a whore. It is hardly my fault that the seed was not sewn in fertile ground. And now I still have a weakling and a whore on my hands."

"Renny is no whore, milord," she bristled.

"I was referring to you. No, something will have to be done about that hair of hers, or she won't even make that. No man will have her. She resembles a boy. On second thought, I know a few men who would prefer that."

"Have you married another weakling, my lord, or do you mean your own daughter?"

"Adele seems hale enough. We'll see how she births when the time comes. You know very well that my Elyse is as addle-pated as your bastard girl is lumpy-headed."

"You know very well she is yours, also. Perhaps I switched the babes. Perhaps I hold the legitimate daughter while you hold the imposter," Maisie challenged.

"Hardly," he responded. "Elyse has both her mother's hooked nose and her temperament. It's unmistakable, although the idea would have been diabolical had you the wherewithal to carry it through."

"Why do you come here? Why do you keep us prisoner?" she asked, changing the subject.

"Mostly because I can. No, in truth, it is your eyes. I want to plumb their depths, possess them. You are interminable to live with but impossible to live without." He reached for her hand, which she withdrew.

"Have you forgotten your word, *mon petite maison?*" She glanced nervously toward the bedroom.

"The child, my lord," she began.

"Had best stay in the rear room. We will be quite all right where we are." He was already unlacing.

She cried out in pain despite herself, trying not to startle the child or give him the added satisfaction of hurting her. Her flinch was as delectable as he had anticipated. He intended to make her flinch again and again. His little bird was ensnared.

22

The moon was shining through the barred window, making trapezoids on the counterpane when the way became clear to her. Why had this not occurred to her before? She knew what he was waiting for. She knew her time was limited, for Renny would come of age quicker than she would like. He would attempt to take Renny when she was ripening. That was an abomination she would not abide. She would murder Renny herself before she would allow that to happen.

She had discovered her way, and it was so painfully obvious. It was so simple, but she would be risking all. If she failed, it would likely mean both their lives. The innkeeper and the balding guardsman had shown small, secretive kindnesses despite being in the employ of the lord. Perhaps they could be enlisted to help, or at least to look the other way when the time came to act.

Lord Clemenceau had taken to sending her gifts of some little value again after his visits. The man was an enigma. Whether he felt some remorse for keeping her as a pet or had some compunction to pay for services rendered, she did not know. She placed the baubles in the selfsame jewel coffer he had once given her, the bottom still strewn with the acorns she had collected from her previous confinement.

Lady Adele bore him a son and survived the ordeal, but the child died within a fortnight. Maisie was left to bear the brunt of his disappointment. He used her cruelly afterwards and she was unable to stifle her cries, which seemed to enflame his rage all the more.

She tried the innkeeper first. He had no love for Clemenceau; that much was clear. He kept his silence with her, but she could hear him rant as he tromped up the stairs, and he cursed the guardsman like they were old friends. She began leaving him little gifts under her napkin. He was sharp. Coinage would appear at the bottom of her soup bowl or baked into her bread. She had cracked her front tooth on the first one but smiled when she realized what she had bitten. She had an ally.

She thought she could trust the balding guardsman as well, but she was unsure of the stocky one. She tested the balding one by dropping a bauble into his lap as she passed while walking to the market. Of course he followed but he remained silent and pocketed the trinket. She hoped he would look the other way.

The second guard, the stocky one, was undoubtedly the informant and reporter of her affairs to the lord. She dropped him some false information, and when Clemenceau inquired whether she might be producing another bastard, she knew with certainty.

Still, the plan was dangerous and would require stomach and courage on both her part and Renny's. She had become convinced the only way to purchase her freedom was with the lord's life, a crime punishable by death, perhaps preceded by torture. Her situation would be irrelevant. The law unfailingly sided with the high-born.

Months passed as she built her plan, stitch by stitch. The smuggling of trinkets in exchange for coin continued right beneath the nose of the stocky guardsman. Finally, she risked a message scrawled by Renny on a tiny scrap of parchment: Book passage.

Three months passed before Renny received a tiny, carved boat from the balding guardsman. The bottom of the carving housed a miniature hinge, inset so that the boat would rest on a flat surface. Maisie used her close work needle to pry open the door. In the nearly invisible cargo hold of the boat was a vial holding the precious droplets of amber liquid. She would need this liquid to subdue Clemenceau. She could never afford enough to kill him, but she could possibly buy herself enough time to act.

The carving had double meaning. She and her daughter would have passage on a trader if they could find their way to Calais. It would take years for them to repay the passage, but limited freedom tasted much sweeter than a lifetime under bolt and key.

The cornerstone for the whole attempt would lie in Clemenceau's ever-present fondness for marchpane. He was a man who adored manipulation. He knew the tray of marchpane was a catalyst for fear. It could just as easily become the thing to catch him unawares. She was indignant she had not devised this plan long ago. She would undo him with his insatiable sweet tooth.

Now, she just had to wait for him to move, or to be moved by some other event that would ignite his hunger for her. The Lady Adele kindly provided the motivation by provoking his aptitude for gloating.

The marchpane-lined tray appeared, and Maisie prepared her daughter for grisly work.

He tromped up the stairs, calling out for her as he climbed. He had happy news. Adele was once again with child. The midwife, ancient now, but wiry and spry, had inspected her womb and declared the growing babe to be the heir. Of course this was nonsense, but Clemenceau wanted so much to believe her predictions that he warmed to the pronouncement. Besides, Adele had already produced one male, albeit weak, so she could do it again.

He reached onto the tray and chose a piece of marchpane. "I'm so elated, I could eat the whole tray," he said as he selected another piece. Maisie tried to appear nonchalant as he downed a third piece of marchpane, still failing to select a single drugged candy.

"Remove my boots, girl; then run along. I have business with your mother." Renny looked sidelong at her mother who nodded imperceptibly. She pulled off Clemenceau's boots and the distinct odor of musty feet filled the room though she dared not comment on it. He was uncharacteristically amiable, even asking after the girl's health of late. His fingers closed around a loaded piece of marchpane, but he hesitated and selected the last clean piece of the almond paste on the tray.

It would be well after he had had his way with Maisie before he would reach for another piece. Renny retreated to the back room to bide her time, taking care not to latch the door, but shutting it hard so that it bounced back, barely ajar.

He treated Maisie tenderly, almost making her question the sanity of what she was about to do. He grabbed another bit of marchpane, choosing to suckle it rather than chew it all at once. He seemed to notice an oddity in the flavor and put it down, half-eaten to choose again. One could never be too careful, although he had never heard of anyone being sickened by marchpane.

He drifted off to sleep. Renny crept silently into the room on bare feet while her mother lay naked beside the sleeping Clemenceau. In her hand, she carried a carved wooden dagger, a finely tipped stake. His rapier lay on the floor beside his breeches, but drawing it would make a distinct noise that would wake him on instinct more than hearing. They could not risk it, though it would have been cleaner.

Maisie laid stock still beside him as Renny approached, arms over her head as she held the stake at the ready. Maisie nodded to her daughter, and Renny drove the stake into Clemenceau's throat. His eyes opened reflexively, and he gasped, flailing. He clouted Renny, and she staggered but held firm to the stake, pushing, pushing.

138

He wrapped his fingers around a handful of Maisie's hair, ripping it from the roots in his struggle. She shrieked and spun off the bed. His mouth opened wide as he attempted to breathe. Maisie grabbed the tray of marchpane and began stuffing it in the gaping hole. Blood oozed from around the stake and a sugary drool trickled out of the corner of his mouth. Lord Clemenceau sputtered and was no more.

"Dress quickly," she ordered her daughter as they doused their hands in the water bowl. Her scalp ached and was probably bleeding, but there was no time to waste. They must away as quickly as possible. She took embers from the brazier and placed them at the four posters of the bed against the bed curtains. The flimsy material caught almost immediately.

They left apace, the door not being bolted when the lord was in house. The stocky guardsman met them at the foot of the stairs, unsheathing his rapier with a growl. They paused, a sword ahead of them, flames behind them, and time seemed to stand still. From behind the guardsman came the innkeeper swinging an iron cook pot. Blood sprayed in an arc from his blow, and the guardsman fell in a heap on the stairs. Maisie and Renny inched past the guardsman as the flames reached the head of the stairs, Renny's finger tracing a pattern along the spattered wall. The innkeeper looked up at the fire licking its way across the roofing beams.

"It is done?" he asked.

"It is done," responded Maisie.

"The horses are saddled. You shall have an escort to Calais. I must sound the alarm, or the blame shall lie at my feet."

The innkeeper rushed out the front of the inn crying "Fire! Fire!" They rushed out the back of the inn to the barn where the balding guardsman was waiting, reins in hand.

As he flung Maisie and her daughter into the saddle, she asked, "Why?"

He grinned and said, "Why ever not?" They were the first words he had spoken to her, and they chilled her to the core. He chirruped, and their horses raced into the night to the fading peal of the alarm bell.

23

The trio set a blistering pace to put as much distance as possible between them and the burning inn. Maisie regretted sacrificing the innkeeper's livelihood, but it had to be done. Her hope was that the belief would be they had all perished in the fire. The one hole in her plan was the guardsman guiding them. He would be missed. It would not be presumed that he, too, would have been abed. If too many questions were asked, it would put both the innkeeper and the balding guard in jeopardy.

She was counting on the Lady Clemenceau to keep silent as she suspected the lord's treatment of her had been as mercurial as his history with both her and his first wife. If she were indeed with child, her future would still hinge on the sex of the baby. But frankly, any future that did not involve Rene Clemenceau had to be brighter. She suspected L'Arbol would not only survive but thrive. She'd had cogs in motion well before her surprise dismissal, and although, it should be hers by might if not by right, she was destined for another direction. When finally they slowed, lest risk losing their mounts, she asked his name.

"Well, that depends."

"On what, Guardsman?" she asked.

"On you. We will need to change our names to avoid detection if Lord Clemenceau's men give chase. And they will demand justice when they discover he wasn't simply the victim of an unfortunate fire. The body count from the ashes won't add up to the number of people known to inhabit the inn. Inquiries will be made."

He took a cloth from his pocket and rubbed the sheen from his bald head. "We need to be married, and hastily."

"I beg your pardon? I thought you were escorting us to Calais, and then we would part ways at the ship."

"What am I going to go back to, aside from a pike? Leaving a post means death. I expect to be compensated for my risk."

"I don't have any money."

"You know, mademoiselle, money is not what I am talking about." Renny shifted, leaning her head against Maisie's back, her breathing settling almost immediately into the rhythm of sleep.

"I will not jump from one prison directly into another," she raised her chin, defiant.

"Don't be a fool. It's the girl you'll want to protect. You'll either board the ship as my wife and child, under my protection, or you'll both be under every man aboard before you reach the New World. The passage is a hard one."

"When we reach the New World, we'll part ways?" If she needed to bed the man to keep her daughter safe, she would, but she didn't want to be saddled with him.

"If you so desire. Of course, after a few months at sea with me, you might be smitten."

"Tell me your name before I agree to this crazed idea."

"It's Beauchene. Jacques Beauchene. And I'll be expecting nightly payments for your safe passage."

"Now it's Clemence. If anyone follows, they will overlook such a closely related name. They will assume I want to get as far away as possible from Clemenceau." She was already thinking ahead. Judging by the looks of him, it would be a small price to pay, and she was willing to invest heavily in Renny's innocence with whatever tender she had at her disposal.

"*D'accord.* What about Christian names?" He was grinning.

"I don't believe there is much that is Christian in this transaction, sir. I shall be Cecille. That is simple enough. You can be Randall and Renny can shift to Renae. I want her name to remain close to the original."

"Why is that, my Cecille?"

"First, she is still a child, and it will prove difficult for her to lie convincingly. More importantly, she is the rightful heir to L'Arbol, and I intend for her to have it."

"An unclaimed bastard and a girl-child?" He was incredulous.

"Oh, I believe one day we'll be able to make a legitimate claim."

"Scheming woman, there is very little legitimate claim about you at all, aside from your prowess under the covers. The cocksure Lord Clemenceau made it widely known, and I am an eager pupil. We will have plenty of time for my lessons on board *The Praying Mantis.*"

"You keep my daughter safe, and you'll get everything you've bargained for, Randall," she said with a smile. He saw her as the victim of Clemenceau's lust, but he failed to recognize her own lust had teeth. L'Arbol would be Renny's one day, she was sure. Maisie only hoped she would be alive to join in her darling Renae's triumph.

Part Three

Daughter

24

Isom and Caro Ballard held tenaciously to a marriage that, for all intents and purposes, existed for the sake of the children, or at least for Brent's sake. Deborah looked for signs of love between her parents but found little to go on. She herself wasn't unhappy as time and routine tend to act as a panacea for a host of slights. She knew her parents' relationship wasn't the norm, but with no experience other than TV sitcoms and her beloved books, it was her norm.

The episode in the pink bedroom faded in her mind to the point that Deborah was no longer convinced it was a memory. Certainly, Mom never made mention of it again, and as time passed, Deborah, on her thirteenth birthday, moved to a larger room on the new wing of the house, leaving her childhood fantasies and her dolls where they hung in that sea of pink. She continued, though, to surround herself with stuffed animals in her new, four-poster bed. Even in her new grownup room, without a swatch of pink, she still awoke as the digital clock read 2:27 a.m. She groaned and turned her back to its glow, but it reflected off the glass of her bay window, like a pair of red eyes.

She had read about circadian clocks and how some people never need an alarm. That scientific knowledge comforted her some, or at least bought her a sense of control on which to cling, although intuitively she knew otherwise. Burying her head in the pillow, she ignored Samson's low growl in the yard below, just as she ignored the niggling sensation of being watched.

July Mountain Boulevard was still a mere avenue of gravel and run-off potholes as Deborah bumped along the road on her Christmas go-cart. She was undersized for her age, the blush of puberty yet to reach her face. Her long, straight hair flew out behind the motorcycle helmet Daddy insisted she wear as she drove. He had souped up the engine so that it would accelerate quickly in case she had to get out of the way of the occasional, crazy, teenaged driver. She roamed over the subdivision roads, with the weeds creeping in from lack of use, and over the old wood trails. She loved motoring along because she could be completely alone. Often, she would park the go-cart beneath a wind-twisted shade tree she found in the meadow on the far side of the mountain. She would munch an apple while looking up at the clouds. She never felt lonely at these times even though she was by herself. She felt loneliest when she was at home. Maybe it wasn't quite lonesomeness. It was more unease, like something bad was coming, and she would be powerless to stop it. Out here, under the gnarly branches that swept the sunlight and clouds into fractal patterns, she could imagine the tree would whisper its story.

Deborah was now old enough to be relied upon to keep Brent in the afternoons after school, and Daddy's regular arrival time began to slide closer and closer to suppertime. The school bus would labor its way up the mountain, drop off the children, and they would be safe while Daddy immersed himself in his own secrets much like Mom hid herself away in a job she didn't need. Daddy said his business provided more than enough.

Daddy almost lost control last night after she came in a full hour after her shift. She claimed to be finishing up her nursing report, and he accused her of sloth on the job. After all, she should be able to plan out her shift so she could care for patients and complete the paperwork. Hell, Daddy cursed, she just sat on her ass for hours watching heart monitors. How hard could it be? She had shot back something Deborah couldn't even remember now, and suddenly her white nurse's cap was flying

147

across the dining room as he grabbed her by her hair, the knot she wore it in providing the perfect hold. Her head was wrenched back, and his other hand was raised to strike when Deborah rattled the door to break the tension. Her nightgown was almost diaphanous in the light, the buds of breasts just visible. Daddy froze, and Mom said, "Go back to bed, Deborah…" just as calmly as if she had been sitting down for a cup of coffee. "And put that back where you found it."

In her left hand she clutched Mom's pocketbook, its secret tucked safely inside. Daddy's eyes drifted down toward Deborah's waist. She was not wearing panties under her nightgown. The light caught the silhouette of her legs and rump as she turned in silence down the hallway. Just like that, the fight was over. Just like that, a new fight had begun.

As Deborah walked toward her room, she opened the purse and fingered the cool lines of the small revolver Mom kept tucked away in the side pocket. She had no intention of using it. She didn't even know how to shoot the thing, but she knew Mom had kept it a secret from Daddy. Its receipt lay buried deep inside the Proof Drawer. She thought she heard Mom call for her purse, but she must have been mistaken. Deborah dropped it on the bench at the top of the stairs where she normally kept it and padded off to lie obediently in bed. She would not drift into sleep for hours, when she was sure the house was quiet, and the danger had evaporated.

As it was well past bedtime, Deborah was thankful Brent would remain oblivious to the late night standoff, just like he was oblivious to the lack of love in the Ballard home. He was showered with affection by both Mom and Daddy, and he failed to notice that the affection came separately. Brent was easy to read. Deborah knew not only that he held nothing but contempt for her, but she also knew why. Deborah was too quiet, too bookish, too bossy, and she was a shrimp. He was finally big enough to give her back some of her own medicine when Mom and Daddy weren't around to save her. He had a growth spurt that left him not only bigger than his older sister, but he also towered over his classmates. Daddy said he was going to be a football star as soon as he grew the rest of the way into his feet. Deborah had just laughed and said, "The bigger the feet, the bigger the stink." Brent made it perfectly clear that he hated the fact that she was in charge during the afternoons before Daddy got home. No girl was ever going to tell him what to do, especially not a shrimpy sister who always looked like she was half-spooked.

25

Deputy Barnevelder chuckled to himself as he stepped onto the school bus. He had just run the new driver, a dried-up, hoarse-voiced, old bag who looked like she'd lived the last thirty years on nothing but cigarettes and coffee, through the safety checkpoints and was ready to guide her through the new route she'd drive come Monday. He had been in charge of school bus driver training for several years now. It wasn't much of a second job, but he told his kids it kept them in pizza money for just doing his God-given duty anyway. He had gotten the spot just after that tornado had cleaned out Woods Cove years ago, and poor old Ivan Johnson, who had trained drivers for decades, was found in the bottom of a pile of rubble that used to be his doublewide trailer.

In the past, he'd always put a male driver on the Woods Cove route, but this new women's lib shit had finally reached Scottsboro, and to his way of thinking, if they wanted to be equals, then they'd just have to do an equal job. He had no doubt she could handle the rowdy Woods Cove boys, but he was looking forward to her face when she wheeled that ten-ton cheese wagon off the top of July Mountain. The last trainee had sweat running down his face on the trip up the mountain, so Barnevelder was pretty sure he wouldn't be able to shove a needle up this woman's ass with a sledgehammer when the time came. Of course, he didn't mean the old lady any harm, and he would show her the spots on the mountain road where she could feather the brakes to keep them from overheating. It was going to be a fun afternoon, but they needed to get moving if they were going to make it back to the schoolhouse by sunset. He had to admit, even he didn't cotton to the idea of taking a bus off July Mountain in the dark.

***

The afternoon was unseasonably warm. It was one of those late February days that promises spring while it still has one foot back in winter. Although Deborah and Brent were required to stay in the house during the interval between school and Daddy getting home, the balmy breeze was just too pleasant to ignore. Besides, Daddy had been coming home later and later. They could enjoy the outside air and be back in the house well before he got home. If they didn't go out now, they would miss a perfect day. They had already been cooped up at school. Why should they stay cooped up now? Daddy would never know the difference anyway.

"I'm going for a walk," Deborah announced as she threw her backpack up the stairs.

"Then, I'll tell," Brent sassed as he tossed his backpack down the stairs toward the den and his beloved video game console.

"Not if you go out, too." Samson had wormed his way into the foyer, curling himself up in a "C" so that both children could pet him at once.

"See, Samson wants to play. Don't you want to play?" Samson wiggled his stub for good measure.

"Okay. But if you make me mad, I'm still gonna tell."

Deborah tossed her ponytail and looked her little brother dead in the eye. "If you tell, I'll tell about that naked picture you've got hid in your room, and you'll get your ass tore up for being a little pervert. Now take Samson, and go play."

151

Deborah was already trotting down the driveway, triumphant. When she got to Daddy's hunting truck, she climbed into the cargo bay, bounced, and let out a whoop.

"You stay in the yard, Brent, and I'll be back in a little while!" She was almost giddy with the excitement.

She eyed the garage and considered hopping on the go-cart, but that would be taking things too far. She had plenty of daylight left if she jogged. Deborah bounded off the back of the truck and took off for the meadow. At the edge of the yard, she turned and hollered, "Hey, Brent! I've got a new nickname for you...." She paused for effect. "Little P! Get it, Pervey?" Brent gave her the finger in return but held onto Samson's collar as she sprinted down the road.

Deborah cut through the woods, dodging trees, and jumping undergrowth as she ran toward her gnarly tree. Although it was warm, it wasn't warm enough for snakes, so she ran without fear. It might be warm enough for the tree to start putting out new growth though, and she was hoping to take this as a sign of spring. She didn't know why this was important to her, but it was almost as if she were being drawn to the tree. She knew there would be hell to pay if Daddy found out she was traipsing through the woods without anyone knowing what she was up to, but she felt the invincibility that comes with being thirteen and on the cusp of full-blown adolescence.

She arrived winded and fell in a heap at the base of the twisted tree. A quick glance up at the branches revealed no new growth, and she sighed at the thought of at least one more cold snap before winter would lose its hold on the mountain. The clicking of the branches had a lulling effect, and the breeze had taken on a chill as the afternoon sun began its descent. She knew as long as she was home before dusk, and she could coerce Brent into keeping his mouth shut, Daddy would be none the wiser. Mom wasn't even a concern as she would be working her hospital shift. Deborah wondered why she hadn't thought of this earlier, why she had wasted all those afternoons being

152

lonely in her room when she could have come here to this part of her mountain instead.

She sat up. Something shifted in her mind, and she recognized a voice so real it was audible. Mom called her Renae Clemence, and Deborah turned instinctively toward the tree to listen more intently. The wind picked up, scraping twigs and limbs against each other in a disjointed cacophony. The roots twisted in the ground beneath her, and Deborah sensed their entrapment and felt entrapped herself. She turned at the sound of a footfall and shuddered to face what was neither flesh nor apparition.

Clemence was kneeling in front of her, searching Deborah's face with bony hands. Scraggly hair covered one eye and plunged to the waist. Pieces of it stood up in matted tufts forming a macabre halo around the wizened face. It undulated with the breeze, and Deborah found herself looking into a mirror of her own ancient self. With breath that stank of earth, age, and rot, Clemence spoke.

"Debbie, Deb, Deborah..." she said in a hiss, "I know you. I have watched you. You forget. You forget what you can do, and your mother hides you from your legacy just like her mother hid her from hers. But I don't forget. I have never forgotten. Yes, my child, this is your mountain. Your mountain has my eyes. You have my eyes. We shall not be forsaken."

Deborah tried to turn her head from the stench of death emanating around her, but the bony fingers held her by the chin. The voice was so close it could have been coming from inside her, but the odor was too distinct to be a fantasy. There was something else, too. Deborah heard a faint droning; she could feel its vibrations in her back as she pressed herself against the tree. It was like that of a carpenter bee, only larger, or maybe more distant. She couldn't really concentrate. The breath was blanketing her like a fog.

"What do you want?" she managed.

153

"I want what's mine. I want your mother to suffer as I have. I want you to suffer as I have. I want what you kept from me when he was in my grasp. I want to taste your pain when your time comes. I want the legacy I was promised."

"I don't understand," Deborah whimpered. The droning sound seemed to grow closer and then fade, as if it were on a circuit.

"That's your mother's doing. You are doubly guilty, for your blood courses both Clemenceau and Ballard. I have whispered the truth to you for years...through the trees, through your dollies, through the mountain itself, and you have ignored me." Clemence stroked the trunk of the tree. "This, my *L'arbre beauchêne*, is the final witness to my vengeance, and it shall bind us in its roots just as we are bound in blood."

"Leave me alone!" Deborah screeched as she sent Clemence sprawling. She stole a quick glance toward home. Clemence was on her again almost immediately, pinning Deborah to the tree.

"There's no one to help you, girl. You are going to have to do for yourself!" Clemence shrieked. "No Clemenceau daughter has stopped me yet, and I'll be damned if you will. I will have what's mine, and I will have him now."

The smell of death was almost overpowering, but all Deborah could think about was that sound. Then it registered. It was her go-cart. Brent was driving the go-cart.

Clemence's eyes shifted from blue to gray, and she tossed her bedraggled hair in glee. "My wait for an heir is over again, and you're lollygagging beneath a tree. What say you we make a sport of it? Do you want to save your brother, gal? You'd better *fly*."

In an instant, Deborah was alone with nothing but the branches of the tree clacking their solitary song. The scent of rot lingered, however, and Deborah sprang into action. Sprinting toward home, she ran faster than she had ever run before, but her feet never left the ground no matter how she willed, wished, or prayed. The breeze strengthened as she cleared the meadow and attempted to cut through the woods to get home faster. Limbs slapped her face and roots broke her momentum, but she kept a driving pace. She had lost the ability to fly if she'd ever really had it at all. Somehow the real memories and the imaginary ones had blended together as she grew up. She felt grown up now as she raced toward her brother. The unmistakable sound of a school bus dropping into low gear, as it climbed the upper incline of the mountain, sent terror pulsing through her, and she motored through the woods at breakneck speed, mindless of suckers and briars snatching at her pumping legs.

Her mind was in slow motion while her body sped. She could see what was about to happen, the scenario unfolding plainly in her head. The bus—why was a bus coming this late in the afternoon?—was going to top the crest, giving it all its engine could. Brent, hair blowing and whooping, would be gunning the go-cart to feel the roller coaster thrill of topping the crest and speeding down toward the guard rail. He was going to be run down!

***

"Okay," Barnevelder instructed, "You're doing fine. You just have this last steep grade to climb. Gear her down all the way now, just before you start the grade. The engine will whine, but you need that extra juice to take you to the top." The trainee had to navigate a sharp curve, avoid the guardrail, gear down, and be ready to brake immediately at the crest. The last pull had a lip at its peak that created a momentary blind spot for a bus driver. The blind spot only lasted long enough to register, but it was there, and Barnevelder watched her face in the mirror as she concentrated, leaning into the wheel to help the bus make the climb, for that second of panic.

***

Deborah screeched as she burst through an opening and into the road just steps from the yard. Brent was on the crest of the hill, driving toward her, not toward the drop-off. Samson chased him as her brother turned backward and laughed. Deborah trotted into the yard, relief on her face.

Brent yelled, "Watch me, Deb!"

She put her hands on her knees to catch her breath. The last few minutes seemed like a whir, almost unreal, but she heard the school bus coming. She glanced at her new digital wristwatch, a gift from Daddy "just because," and was confused at the reading 02.27 as it had to be closing in on five o'clock.

The moment unraveled. Brent was bearing down on the driveway. Deborah thought, "It's the date. Oh, God, it's not a ....c. It's the date!" The bus topped the crest. Deborah's nostrils filled with skunky rot. Samson stopped in the street and howled. Barnevelder grinned as Lady Driver's mouth dropped. A guttural sound wrenched from Deborah.

26

Brent grinned ear to ear as he sped along the drive in front of the house. Just as he approached the driveway, he slammed on the brakes like he'd seen Deborah do to slide sideways into the entrance. But instead of spinning and coming to a stop, he gunned the go-cart as it slid, hoping to spray Deb with dust and gravel as he sped by on the circuit. Brent looked back, laughing at his sister as she was enshrouded in dust.

The cart accelerated faster than he intended, gaining immediate purchase on the drive. In an instant, Brent slammed the cart directly into the back bumper of Daddy's hunting truck. He never even thought to touch the brake.

The sound was as loud as a gunshot. Deb screamed "Stop!" but she knew it was hopeless. She couldn't breathe. She couldn't think. The dog was barking, Brent was sliding, and then there was that sudden double shot. The first shot was the go-cart's steering wheel catching the bumper. The second followed almost immediately and was the sound of Brent's head meeting the bumper as the cart came to an abrupt halt. The force threw Brent headlong into the bumper, snapping his neck as if it was a twig.

His body recoiled from the whiplash effect, and his head slumped to the ground, twisted at an unnatural angle. For the briefest of seconds, for eons of frozen time, the cart's engine screamed. The back tires spun, kicking up a spray of gravel. Her brother's foot slid slowly off the accelerator.

"Brent!" she screamed and the symphony of noise, feeling, and knowledge separated itself. The engine sputtered and quit. Samson barked like a dog possessed, running an invisible enemy out of his yard. She heard another sound, the squeal of brakes. And then, everything went silent as she sank beside her dead brother, the gravel gashing her knees and palms, scraping the side of her face as her world went black.

***

The scent of the thing maddened Samson as he chased it out of the yard, away from his girl. He ran directly in the path of the oncoming school bus. Confused, he grandstanded, facing down the terror he could see rather than chasing one he couldn't.

"What the hell's wrong with that dog?" Barnevelder pointed as the nose of the bus leveled. "Stop, don't run the damn thing down!"

The new driver stood on the brake, slamming him into the door lever before he could steady himself.

"Sorry," she said, and her eyes followed the dog as it turned tail and ran up a driveway, rump tucked under. "Oh, my God...the children!"

Deputy Barnevelder flung the door to the bus open and was on the ground in a single bound. He slid around the front of the bus and knew immediately Brent Ballard was dead. The boy was slumped in a sort of fetal position on the driveway. His head was thrown against his back, eyes open, a red smear across his forehead. The impact had peeled back his scalp. Gray matter soaked into the gravel in an oily stain. It was too late for this poor boy.

His sister lay face down on the driveway, whimpering. The dog lapped at the boy's face, cleaning the blood from his eyes which had already begun to sink in their sockets.

158

"Get away!" He kicked at the dog, who retreated under the truck with a whine. The lady bus driver vomited in the grass. It was a hell of a training session.

"Deb, Little Debbie." He took the girl into his arms. "It's me, Deputy Barnevelder. I'm here. I've got you. Help is on the way." She was shocky but did not seem to be seriously injured.

"I couldn't stop her," she sobbed. "I couldn't stop her." She tried to wriggle from the deputy's grasp.

"No. Don't look. He's gone. He's already gone." Barnevelder cradled the girl, lifting her up and away from the scene.

"Get back to the bus and call the ambulance on the bus radio," he said to the bus driver. He knew she wouldn't be driving this route tomorrow or any other day. She ran to the bus.

He carried the girl into the house, up the stairs, and paused to survey the surroundings. He took her to the living area on his left, well out of the line of vision of the scene in the driveway. He saw an afghan folded over the back of the sofa and wrapped her gently in it. Her long hair hung limply, tangling in the folds of the afghan. She was bleeding from the scrapes, but those would clean up easily enough.

"Stay here, Little Debbie. I'm getting help," he said gently. She shook so violently he couldn't tell whether she nodded assent. He quickly stepped into the hall and tried the hall closet. Cleaning supplies. He strode to the first room. It was the boy's bedroom, a Star Wars bed sheet in a wad on the unmade bed. He grabbed the sheet and took the stairs two at a time.

Back in the driveway, he gingerly placed the sheet over the dead boy, trying not to see the awkward bend of the neck, the fold of scalp rooted with sodden hair. He called the dog, who growled at him from his place beneath the truck.

"Keep this dog away from the child," he called to the driver who was slumped, sobbing, over the steering wheel of the bus. He could hear a siren faintly in the distance. An ambulance was climbing the mountain.

159

He ran back inside the house and found the telephone on the kitchen wall. He dialed the hospital switchboard. "This is Deputy Barnevelder. Put me through to the emergency room immediately."

When the attendant answered, he said, "Caro Ballard is nursing in the intensive care unit. Get the crash cart ready for her. I'm bringing in her children. It's bad."

He hung up and rummaged through the kitchen drawer, looking for a phone book. He didn't see one and then noticed Ballard's magnetic business card was stuck to the refrigerator door, along with an assortment of grade school art and spelling quizzes. Brent made good marks. So did his sister. He dialed the number on the card. There was no answer. He glanced at his watch. It was five minutes past five o'clock. Ballard must already be driving home. He might even follow the ambulance on his way.

Barnevelder went back to the couch and held the girl. The ambulance horn blew moments later, urging the school bus out of the way.

He kissed her on the forehead and told her to sit tight for just a few more minutes. He rushed down the stairs and out the door.

"What do we have, Deputy?" the EMT swung out of the ambulance while his partner began unpacking equipment. They were deliberate, not hurried as they had been trained to be.

"Looks like the boy drove his go-cart up under the truck. Neck's broken. Probably instant."

The EMT pulled back the sheet covered in little Darth Vaders.

"Mother of God," he grimaced. "He near about decapitated himself." He replaced the sheet. "Call the coroner, Ted. We've got a DOA."

The EMT put a hand on Brent's shoulder and said, "I'm sorry, kid." He looked to Barnevelder. "Dammit. It still gets to me when it's a kid."

"His sister's in shock. I took her into the house so she wouldn't see. She'll need tending to."

"I'll get the kit," he said. "You know these folks?" the EMT asked.

His nametag identified him simply as Tommy, like he was a gas station attendant rather than an ambulance driver.

"Yeah, it's the Ballard kids. You probably seen their mama, the pretty, silver-haired nurse who works in intensive care. You know the one. Their daddy owns that hunting supplies store in the new shopping strip out toward the river. From the looks of this house, he may own the strip, too."

"Damn," was all the EMT had to say as he followed Barnevelder into the house.

The coroner arrived within minutes and pronounced the Ballard boy dead. Brent was loaded into the ambulance and transported directly to the funeral home. No autopsy would be necessary. The new school bus driver got hold of her husband and he came to get her, leaving the bus where it stood in the road. Little Debbie was taken by ambulance to the hospital where both she and her mother were sedated. Deputy Barnevelder stayed behind, waiting on Ballard to arrive home. It was well after six p.m. and turning colder by the minute. It looked like their little bit of Indian summer was over. Ballard had not called the house to check on his children. He was not answering at the store. A squad car had been sent to retrieve him, but he seemed to have disappeared.

The dog had run off, too, or at least moved out of sight. Barnevelder hosed down the driveway himself, thinking it a mercy to clean up the mess so that Ballard's wife would not see the wreckage. He wheeled the go-cart, its steering column bent, to the garage, but then had another idea when he saw Ballard's garden tractor with the key sitting in it.

He grabbed some chain he saw lying about and cinched the steering column to the auger on the back of the tractor. He fired up the tractor, raised the auger gently and backed the go-cart out

161

of the garage. He put the tractor in gear and hauled the cart—its front wheels lifted—over the rise and down the first incline. He edged the tractor to the spot where the guardrail came to a premature end and lowered the auger. He unlashed the steering column and heaved the go-cart over the drop-off. The incline was so steep, the cart tumbled as it crashed through the underbrush to the littered mountain floor below. Beer cans, tossed over the guardrails, glinted in the tractor's beams as he buried the go-cart in the mass of underbrush and runoff caused by the steepness of the slope. He considered the act one of respect for Caro, who had nodded her assent when he asked if she could ease his grandmamma's suffering when she was lying in intensive care, eaten up with cancer. He didn't know if she actually did anything, but his grandmamma had gone to be with Jesus before the night was out. He could do this thing to ease her pain.

Barnevelder rode the tractor back to its place in the garage. There was still no sign of Ballard, but he knew he must return soon. He turned on the porch lights and sat at the slider in the dining room while he waited. He could be out in the driveway to meet Ballard by the time the son of a bitch parked his car. He felt a little sorry for him, though. His son lay dead in the funeral home while he was probably making a run out past the county line for a case of beer.

Headlights glowed through the pines at last, and Ballard's car slowed as he approached the driveway, a school bus oddly out of place in the road. Barnevelder rushed out the door to meet Ballard.

"What the hell are you doing here?" Ballard barked, already three sheets to the wind.

"Waiting on you, Mr. Ballard. Something terrible's happened. We need to get to the hospital."

"What? Where are my kids? Deb? Brent? What has happened?"

"How about you let me drive? Slide on over, Ballard. I'll get you there as quick as I can."

27

It was the second funeral Deborah had attended, and it was wrenching. Her father fell to his knees, burial side, sobbing against the casket, which looked oversized for a child Brent's age. Deborah's mother stood stock still, whether stoic or sedated, or a little of both, Deborah did not know. Deborah's grandmother, who might as well have been a stranger, Nonny, stood beside her, constantly dabbing at her eyes with a tissue even though her eyes were dry. Her only grandson had not even made it to his tenth year. Deborah was not sure he would even know who their grandmother was if he could see her now. As people filed by the casket to offer their final respects and take the traditional rose for remembrance, Nonny put her hand possessively on Deborah's shoulder.

"You'll be coming home with me, Deborah. We have important matters to discuss, you and I."

Mom spoke low and with venom, "You haven't spoken to me in seven years, and you want to take my only living child from me now?"

"That's your doing, Caroline. The phone rings both ways. The road drives in both directions. Don't even pretend you've made an effort since Levin died. You know it must be done. We must put a stop to this pain once and for all. My heart can't take any more." Nonny's voice was calm, deliberate.

Mom merely nodded.

"I don't want to go," Deborah whispered.

"You'll do as you're told," Mom hissed and turned back to the casket. She had ordered the floral blanket in black orchids interspersed with white roses. It was beautiful but harsh in black and white. She had wanted it to be reminiscent of the space characters Brent had loved so dearly. But as friends, family, and even strangers filed by, Deborah noticed that they only plucked the roses. The casket darkened as mourners filed past. A southern funeral, especially one for a child, will bring out all sorts of folks you didn't even notice cared about you. Folks who might not even give you the time of day if they saw you on the street will turn out for a child's funeral.

Deborah took their hands blindly as she watched the white roses disappear from the funeral spray, to be pressed into scrapbooks and collected in hope chests, as a reminder that life is fleeting, that no one is immune. She hoped they remembered her brother, or perhaps said a prayer for those he left behind. One by one, the people removed the metaphor of innocence from the casket, and as each rose was plucked, Deborah watched her mother sink under the weight of grief even as she willed herself erect. Her father's arm was draped around Mom's shoulder, holding her in place but adding to the weight. His eyes were focused somewhere beyond the tented burial area. The vague outline of a flask was almost invisible in the pocket of his sport coat. Nonny had Deborah cinched at the waist, clinging to her with a grip that made Deborah feel trapped and a bit lightheaded.

The orchids, exotic and heady, shrouded Brent in darkness even before he was placed in the ground. Their scent overpowered the roses but could not quite disguise the smell of earth yawing beneath the hideous and worn green carpet marking the grave. The funeral attendants could not seem to get the awful carpet to spread flat, and its folds created a tripping hazard for all who took the graveside stroll, plucking roses and muttering words that stabbed instead of comforted. The upholstery covering the family viewing chairs, now abandoned—as what was left of her family stood to view the grim parade—was also worn, its green, plush fabric faded and crushed from overuse. Deborah wondered how often the funeral people had used the same equipment and props, how many heartbroken families had sat in those very chairs. Were they bored with the routine of it all? She wondered how many other sisters had once saved their baby brothers only to let them die.

The orchids were pungent, obscene in their perfumed demands. Deborah thought about her tree, standing sentinel all those years ago and falling to protect her and a baby Brent from a wicked storm. She had always been able to recognize the smell of death, and now she had learned the smell of despair. It clung to her parents as surely as those orchids clung to Brent's casket. Her grandmother's vice-like grip around her waist claimed her, and Deborah leaned into Nonny, choosing an unknown future over one of such utter sadness. She sensed her parents were through. They had nothing left to hold them together, especially not her. She had let him drive the go-cart. She didn't stop him. They blamed her, maybe even wished it was Deborah in the casket instead of Brent. Their graveside embrace was as cold and empty as Mom's eyes as she prepared to bury whatever love she had left in her with Brent.

At last, the macabre parade came to an end, and nothing was left but to turn and walk into the church basement where there would be a different sort of reception while the workers lowered Brent into the waiting earth. A backhoe stood at the ready, discreetly parked behind an azalea bush. In the distance, she heard the peal of laughter as a small girl leap-frogged over a tiny headstone with a lamb engraved on it. The little girl had no idea what grief was, but she would. She would.

***

They drove in silence back up the mountain and into the driveway, Nonny following behind in her sedan. Emptiness clung to Mom, wrapped around her like a shroud. She was utterly defeated, devastated.

"I'll never ride in that truck again," she said flatly. "Get rid of it. I don't want to see it."

"It takes some time to sell a vehicle. We won't be able to sell it around here. Everyone will know," Daddy replied as he fished under the seat for a bottle.

"I don't care if you drive it off the cliff. Just get it away from me." She got out and turned on Nonny, who had just pulled up. "Don't park there! Don't you ever park on that spot!"

Nonny backed up a respectable distance and got out. "I am sorry, Carolyn. Let's go inside. I'll make some coffee, and we can get Deborah packed up. She shouldn't see you like this."

Nonny led Mom into the house, barely nodding to Daddy who mumbled something about going to the garage. Her grandmother walked her mother up the steps and set her down at the dining room table, treating her like the guest in her own house. Mom was too numb to do anything but obey. Deborah watched as Nonny navigated the kitchen as if it were her own. She knew precisely where everything was located even though this was the first time she had set foot in their house.

"Go get a suitcase from under the stairs and take it to your room, Deborah. I will be in to help you pack your things in just a minute." Deborah glanced over at Mom who was sitting slumped like a rag doll in the chair. Their eyes met, and any final hope of forgiveness or love was washed away. The percolator plunking its syncopated raindrops and the fragrance of fresh coffee almost masked the faint odor of earthy rot and sickly sweet orchid that clung to her mother.

Deborah wrestled the suitcase down the hall as her mother and grandmother drank coffee. She paused at Brent's doorway, looking in at the cluttered mess of a boy's room. It had remained untouched since the accident, Star Wars toys and a half-finished puzzle from last Christmas willy-nilly on the desk and floor. Dirty cleats had leeched red clay onto a carelessly

167

tossed bath towel, and an open bag of chips had scattered on the unmade bed. It really looked like Brent would return any moment and maybe even make good on his promise to Mom to clean his room. It was all over. Deborah slipped over to his chest of drawers and dug around for his naked woman picture. She pocketed it. The least she could do was keep his secret. Deborah silently closed the door to his room and lugged the suitcase to her own.

After shoving some junk in the suitcase, Deborah wandered back to her room—not her new grownup room, but the pink one. She half-expected the dolls to talk to her, to tell her what to do. She half-expected the mirror to show her Clemence, her grandmother ageless, as Mom had called her, with her hair unbound and whipping in the wind. But they were silent. Perhaps they had never even spoken at all. After all, it had been so long ago, and Mom had never again mentioned their conversation; maybe it never really happened. She had swallowed it all down and kept it locked deep inside just like her mother had told her to do. People weren't supposed to know what she knew or see what she had seen. It was dangerous, and what good was it anyway? She couldn't save Brent, and in not being able to save Brent, she had killed her mother. Oh, she was sitting in the kitchen sipping coffee, but she was dead just the same. Deborah knew it, Nonny knew it, and even Daddy probably knew it if he could clear his head of the booze. That's why Nonny was taking her away, and maybe that was for the best.

Deborah was working all of this out in her head as she stared in the antique mirror. The dolls, hanging in their places on the wall, could just go hang for all she cared. They had not served to defend the family against squat. It was all just silly rot, so were her dreams, and so was the idea of a grandmother eternal. Her real grandmother was in the next room, tiptoeing around Mom. She was real, and she was Deborah's ticket out of a house that had fallen apart. Brent's accident didn't rip Mom

168

and Daddy apart. They had already done that for themselves. Mom, despite all her so-called fears, was drowning herself in work, and Daddy was drowning himself in a bottle. They had been so pre-occupied with themselves that they hadn't even noticed. Hell, Brent was probably the lucky one in all of this. At least he wouldn't have to watch their lives tumble down. At least he wouldn't have to spend his life afraid of what he would see in the mirror.

Deborah cried as she folded the contents of her suitcase neatly rather than dumping them in willy-nilly as she had first done. She cried for Brent, and she cried for the illusion of family. She cried for her mother, who had spent years resolutely pushing her away, because she knew the same rejection was playing out over cups of coffee and an army of tin-foiled casserole dishes covering every inch of the kitchen countertop. She knew the chasm had stood open between them for years, bridged only by a worn newspaper article with a faded photo of a silver-haired woman with a child in hand.

Deborah turned from the bulging suitcase, so out of place on the pink-flounced bed, and faced her mirror, a mirror where no images appeared but her own. Had they ever? She stared hard at the reflection, not a carbon-copy, but a derivative of her mother and her mother's mother. Had they been standing side by side, they might very well have appeared to the casual observer at different stages of the same life, almost like a time-lapsed photograph. Their similarities were striking, especially their fine, gossamer hair. Deborah fingered her hair, wrapping it tightly and watching it fall back into place, stick-straight almost to her waist. Her eyes were swollen with crying, but she could see clearly enough as she took the scissors out of the top right drawer and cut chunks out of her hair. The hair fell to the floor around her feet and looked for all the world like spider webs glistening in a forest of pink shag.

No more tears would fall from her eyes—not for her brother, not for her mother, not for herself. She slipped Brent's

169

favorite baseball cap, the one she had hidden away as payback for whatever bratty thing he had done last week, over her shaggy head and zipped the suitcase. When her grandmother came at last to the door, she was ready.

Epilogue

Our names define us and our names cling to us. They cling to our daughters and granddaughters like cobwebs cling to a corner. We may sweep them aside, but they will stick to the very broom, binding themselves to the fibers. They bind us. They heal us. They destroy us. We use them purposefully to define our work, like the names Smith and Wright. We use them to define where we are from, like the names Park and London. We use them to define to whom we belong, like Johnson or Fredrickson. We use names to describe some quality of our nature, or the nature of those before us, like Savage or Angel. We use names to stake our place in time or mark popular trends, like Tiffany or Elizabeth. Our names evoke meaning, and our names invoke meaning. Our names transport us, and our names can transcend time. Our names become the taproot of generations.

They say the sins of the fathers can be brought down on the head of a seventh son of a seventh son. The sins of the mothers, however, can be passed down world without end. And aren't they the same sins, just played out in different ways? And aren't they the same names, just lived out time and time again? Time is not merely linear. To think so is folly. Time is cyclical. It is kinetic. It is a trinity. And sometimes, all that is needed to transcend it all is a grand old name.

About the Author

Rocky Porch Moore spent her formative years atop July Mountain, overlooking picturesque Scottsboro, Alabama. She completed her undergraduate work at the University of Alabama and earned her Master's at the University of South Alabama, both in Secondary Education Comprehensive Language Arts as well as earning NBPTS National Board Certification in Adolescent and Young Adult Reading and Language Arts. Teaching since 1991, Rocky has earned recognition numerous times. She was most recently honored with the University of Alabama Office of Research on Teaching in the Disciplines Excellence in Teaching Award (2014). She currently teaches a variety of high school language arts courses.

Rocky has served as an occasional contract curriculum writer, penning standardized test practice questions, novel study guides, and developing content for the ALSDE Introduction to Journalism ACCESS online curriculum. She is the author of a children's book, *It's Farm Market Day!* (2009).

Rocky and her husband of twenty-four years live on a farm in Foley, Alabama, where they are raising four children, a herd of Texas Longhorns, a pair of Great Danes, and a plethora of farm animals. She enjoys reading, running, and cooking.

173

CPSIA information can be obtained at www.ICGtesting.com
Printed in the USA
BVOW02s0035150116

432938BV00003B/25/P